Jerri Locke

Copyright © 2014 Jerri Locke
All rights reserved
First Edition

PAGE PUBLISHING, INC.
New York, NY

First originally published by Page Publishing, Inc. 2014

ISBN 978-1-62838-930-2 (pbk)
ISBN 978-1-62838-931-9 (digital)

Printed in the United States of America

PRELUDE

My name is Jerri Locke, I am forty-two years of age, and I am over filled with joy as I present to the world my first novel. I have always loved poetry and had written several poems that kept turning into short stories. As I was attempting to turn the title of this novel into a poem, I surprised myself when I stopped rhyming and the story kept going. Before I knew it, I had outlined a story with a message that I felt everyone needed to hear.

First of all, I want my readers to know how this story came to me. It all started with a quote that I used to try and get through to my daughter, Lakeisha Johnson. Lakeisha is the oldest of my three daughters. She is a beautiful twenty-five-year-old woman with a beautiful spirit. Although she knows the path she must take, she has a way of going overboard to express her opinions, especially to me. She can be as humble as a pleasant lamb to as angry as a raging bull in moments.

One day while I was going along with my daily activities, she showed up at my house on one of her "you better get right" missions. Lakeisha's goal had become saving souls, which was great. However, she never once thought that, if she humbled herself, she may easily get her point across.

Anyway, that day, she started out peaceful, but she can't stand any opposition; so if you don't agree with her every word, peace is short lived. Being that I'm the momma, I couldn't help but disagree with some of her statements, which led to her disrespect. When she refused to back down and felt the need to make others, including me, feel down, I told her that "I would rather go to hell than the heaven that you're in."

Keisha then looked at me as if her eyes were going to pop out of her head and shouted "Are you crazy? You are sending your soul to hell." When I responded that if heaven is where she's going, I chose hell. She walked away quietly. Walking away is not often done by my child, so it felt good.

For several weeks following our conversation, I could not shake this quote from my mind. I didn't want it to be a bad thing, so I meditated on how to express myself better. Since I had started my second poetry book titled *She Snapped*, I figured I would put this poem in it. As you can see, it never made it to a poem. During these weeks, I talked about this troubling quote to several of my clients at JC Penney hair salon. While talking with them, I came up with a story to describe my feelings about this quote. The more questions they asked, the deeper my story got.

I then joked with myself and said I might as well write a novel. One client asked me the question, "Who would it be about?" That's when I came up with the evangelist Catalina. I then decided to use Zonita to tell the story. You are about the find out that the story went much deeper than Evangelist Catalina.

Finally, I used my knowledge from my grandparents and others around me to add a little old-time wisdom to the novel. Most of the sayings in this story came to me from my grandmother Elizabeth. Most called her Liz. In my first poetry book called "She Got Issues," I wrote a poem titled "She Bad." This poem describes my legendary grandmother and her humorous but wisdom-filled sayings. In this novel, they are called Big Belle's rhymes or sayings. Now some of them came from me, and I've decided to let my readers guess which ones.

I'm sure that I've given you enough information to know that the poetry in this novel comes from me. It felt gratifying to write this story and incorporate my love of poetry in it in various ways. There are song lyrics that I made up also throughout the novel.

Overall this was an experience of a lifetime. I hope to write more novels, but if I don't, I have accomplished something that I never dreamt of. I wrote my story, and if it does not touch several hearts, it did touch one, mine.

INTRODUCTION

My name is Zonita Labelle Walker. I am named after my maternal grandmother Labelle Walker. I never understood why they called her Big Belle; she was a short, skinny woman since I've known her. Anyway, she instilled in me her knowledge, wisdom, and her pride. Well, at least she tried. She often told me that I was her healing child. You see, my mother died when I was two, leaving my grandma to raise me. As I grew looking like my momma, she told me that I helped her heart heal.

My mother was one of nine siblings. However, there was only one left at home with me, Baby Cat. I remember jealousy and hatred from my aunt, whom I knew was not my sister. I felt like she was, but she made sure that I knew that Big Belle was her mamma not mine. Mine was dead. As a small child, I didn't understand how she could be so hateful.

JERRI LOCKE

I'D RATHER GO TO HELL THAN THE HEAVEN THAT YOU'RE IN

As time went on, Baby Cat and I became as close as any two sisters could be. She taught me all the juicy stuff about life. She was so pretty, and I was determined to be just as beautiful. As a teenager, I often imitated Cat's switching. She was twenty-one and had blossomed into this woman that could easily be on television. Big Belle just rolled her eyes at Cat sashaying around and spit one of her many rhymes, "Kiss what you twist and not my wrist," All the old folks and kids laughed until their faces were drained with tears.

Years passed, Big Belle was gone. Baby Cat became a stranger to me, and I became a stranger to myself. For years, I blamed everyone, especially those close to me, like Cat. Well, I can't call her Cat anymore. Why couldn't life just stay put. Now I find myself praying that I was dreaming. I'm really still a teenager full of dreams.

My choices got me here. Now all I can do is wish that I had chosen a better path for me and my children. My momma died from a dumb drive-by shooting. I wish she hadn't been with that gangster boyfriend; she would have still been alive.

There I go again, blaming the past for my bad choices. I left my children, knowing that I was wrong. I knew the lord was my Shepard, but I couldn't pray to him. I chose the devil for he made my flesh feel good momentarily, but my spirit burned forever.

I don't like it here. I want to see Big Bell and my momma again. All I see is darkness, and all I smell is smoke. How do I get out of this hellhole?

JERRI LOCKE

CHAPTER 1

Baby Cat

"Praise him! Praise him! Praise him in the morning. Praise him in the noon day. Praise him when the sun goes down!"

Big Belle could really blow. The whole church shouted and praised God when she sang. Well, except for Baby Cat. Big Belle is my grandma, but the only mamma I've ever known. She made sure that church was a part of our lives. I loved church, but my aunt Baby Cat had an issue with the fake church folks, as she called them.

"Woman, where is my plate?" yelled Jack. Jack was Big Belle's husband. He is mean as hell, and nobody understands why she married him. They say he ain't never been nothing but a drunken fool. I don't say anything 'cause Big Belle says that the Bible says, "Honor thy parents. Don't ask why or you will die." So being obedient, I took Jack his plate while he sat on the sofa smoking them funky cigars. Every now and then, I swore that I smelt some weed. Those were the days when his eyes were low, and he giggled like he was in a halfway good mood. I bet he got some money 'cause he too ugly to look at, and Big Belle has always been the finest woman in this area. Surely, she's getting more than a stiff ( ) out the deal.

Baby Cat taught me all about those. I can't wait until my first, I thought as Baby Cat and I made our way to the backyard. Every Sunday evening, we would sit on the porch and watch the cute boys ride by. "I don't know why momma cooked all that pork," Baby Cat fussed. "If I keep eating that shit, my ass gone be big as this porch like hers used to be, and that little cutie won't look at me anymore." I just looked at her like, Girl, that pork ain't what's making that butt big. It's that peach cobbler you eating after you high off that weed. I would never say that out loud. I loved her too much to hurt her. Anyway, if her butt got huge, she would blend in with all the new hip-hop stars.

"Come on, Nita. Let's walk. I think I see him." Baby Cat always made me walk beside her while she moved like the waves of the ocean. Since I was kind of unshapely at this time, it made her stand out.

"Hey boo, how you doing?"

"Fine," Cat replied.

Then Darian, the fine boy would slickly say, "I know you fine, but how you doing."

I just chuckled, thinking, Can't he get a new line? That line worked for Darian every time, and I became the lookout girl once again. I could always keep Big Belle from going toward the back.

When it was over, Cat and I would go to bed, and she would tell me romantic stories. She had the perfect dream wedding planned for her and Darian. I listened, hoping that one day I would be having the same dream. First, I have to grow some titties and have my period. I hoped that I'd be built like my momma. Big Belle said that the boys were knocking her door down after my momma. Of course, she only told me that when I was feeling tomboyish. Baby Cat told me the truth. She said that I would get titties when I got old enough for a boy to suck on them. She said that hers went from grapes like mine to grapefruits in no time.

"Nita, wake up! Have you seen my red skinny jeans? I always wear them on Mondays. I look so fly switching around campus in those. I could have sworn they were hanging right here."

Damn, Baby Cat gone be mad if I tell her that she don't have those anymore. I guess I'll just let her believe that she misplaced them. Heck, she can't prove that I had anything to do with them, I thought.

If only I hadn't been trying on Baby Cat's clothes. I wanted to see if I was thick like the boys called her. So one day while she was gone to school, I decided to play dress up. When school started back, I would be a freshman. I figured I needed to be fly too. Unfortunately, I've always been a klutz. While trying to look at my booty in the mirror, I slipped and fell. The jeans fit but were under my feet. I must be a little thick cause I split them skinny jeans from one end to the other. I flew in the living room and nervously asked Big Belle for her sewing kit.

"Nita, what you done did?"

"Nothing, Ma," I replied. "I'm just trying to stitch up some ole doll clothes." Knowing that I was lying, she said it's over there in that top drawer.

I anxiously hurried back to my room and stitched up those pants in minutes. After I finished, there was nowhere to put your legs in the jeans. So my next solution was to burn them up before anyone notices. I did just that. These bad kids down the street were always setting the dumpster on fire. I acted like I had a little trash and tossed them into the burning dumpster.

"Nawl, Cat. I ain't seen yo jeans." I didn't even sound like myself. I hate lying. Big Belle didn't like liars either. She always could catch someone in a lie. "You're lying a sack of shit, and your nickname is Dodo," was one of her famous lines.

So Cat went on to school in some different jeans, and I lay in bed depressed over the lie but relieved that she didn't find out. I was miserable all day. I skipped breakfast, which was unusual for me since Big Belle's slab bacon and homemade biscuits were my favorite. Big Belle still cooked like she was in the ole days. Molasses. Who still eat homemade molasses? I loved it, but my friends thought I was crazy.

They kept tearing up their biscuits, trying to spread it. I laughed 'cause I was a pro at it. It was all we used in our house.

After skipping dinner too, I realized that messing up Baby Cat's jeans had me in a deep depression. I hated seeing her sad. However, I knew that I could never tell her. I was afraid of losing my sister and my closest friend. Besides, I'd seen how she got when somebody did something to her stuff. She hasn't spoken to her ex-bestie, Tamar, since Tamar didn't return her purple bottom wedges for a month. When she got them back, they were black bottoms. She talked about that girl so bad until everybody around cried with laughter, but poor Tamar was humiliated and never returned. After that, every time someone asked Cat to borrow something, she told them about the bitch that messed up her purple bottom wedges. Since I couldn't stand to be humiliated by Baby Cat, I decided to take this one to the grave.

I finally decided to eat a piece of pecan pie with French vanilla ice cream on top. Big Belle and I sat in front of the television, tearing the pie up right in front of Jack's diabetic face. I was sorry that he couldn't have any, but he shouldn't have been so ugly. Anyway, the door slams shut and here comes hell.

Baby Cat is pissed off about something, and when she's pissed, look out! Everybody gone feel her wrath. "What's wrong, Cat?" Big Belle reluctantly moaned.

"Momma, I'm tired. I gots to move from here. I'm twenty-one years old; it's time for me to move out. I needs my space. Can't have no boyfriend overnight 'cause you so damn religious, *fornication* is a sin. If I stay out late, you gets no sleep, and on top of that, my shit coming up missing. I'm moving out."

After that blow up, Cat stormed out and the storm ceased. Then the storm raged in me. What I'm gone do? Cat leaving and I need her. She'll probably never visit. Who gone teach me what to do with my first boyfriend? Who gone help me dress for prom? All my dreams of growing up with her here to show me the way is over. It's all my fault. I shouldn't have messed up her stuff. If she leaves, I'm gone be bad. Big Belle won't be able to handle me. I figured she'd have to come back to help her poor old momma.

I'D RATHER GO TO HELL THAN THE HEAVEN THAT YOU'RE IN

I loved Big Belle, but all she knows is praying to Jesus and going to church. "Who gone take me to the club?" I knew then that everyone would be saying. "Look at that fast girl Zonita. She gone be just like Bonita, her momma."

JERRI LOCKE

CHAPTER 2

Bonita

Big Belle didn't talk much about momma, and Baby Cat was ten when she died. She didn't know much, only rumors that she heard later. The rumors were that my momma was a hot mess. She was beautiful and built like a brick house. Some said she worked at the strip clubs across the water. Other rumors were of her doing all kinds of drugs and sleeping with different men. Cat said that because of my momma, Big Belle would sprinkle oil all over the house. She believed that the evil spirits would stay away.

On several occasions, I would get curious and pick Big Belle's brain about my momma. She would say things such as, "Yo momma was a beautiful, smart girl just like you are." She'd also tell me how my momma was an artist at doing hair and makeup. She said momma would come up with new hair styles before they ever came on magazines. "Honey, I would go to church on Sunday with my hair fried, dyed, and laid to the side. All the ladies at church wanted my hairdo."

Every now and then, while Big Belle was bragging about momma, old Jack would say "Belle, you know that gal was a whore stripper. That one gone be just like her." Big Belle would say, "Don't pay him no attention. That diabetes got him senile." You could tell Big Belle loved her kids. Yes, she was a Christian but never judgmental. Anyway, she lied too! Every time I asked, "Do I have a daddy? Where is he? Who is my daddy?"

"Momma's baby, papes maybe." She said it all my life. You didn't know what she meant by that, but she said it too much. The older I got, the more I wanted her to just tell the damn truth.

This was the very reason I was crazy. My momma was nothing but a dope addict whore; my grandma is a liar; and Baby Cat, she is self-centered. On top of all that, I don't have a daddy. I got the right to be messed up in the mind.

I do wish I could have known my momma. "Bonita Michelle Walker, who are you? Everyone tells me that when they look at me it's the same as looking at you. What happened in your life that caused you to do all the horrible things that you were accused of? Why would I be headed down the same path? Did you know Jesus is a savior? Didn't Big Belle make you go to church like she does us? Well, I'm not gone be like you. I'm going to pray and get saved."

I remember one Sunday evening after church being determined to get some answers about my momma. I got the right to know why God gone punish me. The preacher clearly preached a sermon today, stating that the Bible, which tells no lies, said that your parents' sins can cause punishment to their offspring. Maybe he didn't say it just like that, but that is how I took it.

"Big Belle! Who killed my momma? Why somebody want to take her life? Did you see how she looked as she was dying?"

Big Belle would shout, "My heart can't take this. How many times do I have to tell you the gang people did it because of that boy she was fooling with, and no, I couldn't look nor accept losing my child. I just hold on to you and promise myself that I would never let you go."

I'D RATHER GO TO HELL THAN THE HEAVEN THAT YOU'RE IN

I was a mouthy teenager, so I kept on talking. "Well, where the gangsters at now? I want to talk to them."

I didn't know what I would do if the gangsters came my way, but at that time, I felt like giving somebody a piece of my mind. I was fourteen-years-old and full of rage. When I thought about my momma gone and I didn't have a daddy, I just wanted to fight.

Summer was coming to an end, and it was almost family reunion time. I loved the reunions during the day. It was when everyone came over to sleep and gossip all night that I hated. They always looked me up and down and wondered if I had started doing what grown folks do.

"Nita, turn around! Girl! You know, you got Bonita's shape on you." That's all Aunt Margret ever said. She got on my nerves. She acted like she was a dike or something. "I wish she would keep her eyes off of me." At this time of my life, I was such a smart aleck with little respect. I rolled my eyes and said, "What happened to yours?" Well, I actually mumbled the words so she had to guess what I had said. Big Belle was still dishing out a whooping, and I didn't want one.

Aunt Margret always had something to say about my momma. Maybe she could answer some of my questions, I thought. "Tete!" That's what I say to my aunts when I wanted something. "I love your new car." Compliments always worked.

"What you want, Nita," she snapped. "Nothing. Just wanted to talk about my momma."

"What you wanna know? What don't you know? Big Belle got a whole photo album of her right over there. She thought your momma was her superstar child. Bless her heart, she was so blind. I loved my big sis Bonita, but she was too much. Yes, I've always been the larger sister, and she always downed me saying that I needed to eat salads. She said that I would never get a man if I didn't shape up."

Really! There she goes again every time she came home, she whined about the same ole shit. OK, you're fat. That's not what I asked you. "Awe! Tete, you not fat. You thick. I enjoyed seeing you do the wobble at the reunion. You shut all those skinny girls down. The song says, 'Hey, big girl, back it up. Not hey, skinny girl.'"

"Thanks, boo." She smiled with some confidence.

"Your momma's boyfriend Z was about six foot six and had the silkiest dreads I had ever seen. He always bragged about his big record deal. He said he was going to be signed by Flow Cold Records. Your momma thought that she would be the next video girl. She told me that Z once threw a thousand dollars on her stage when she was dancing at the Red Garter. I felt like they so rich, but Big Belle struggling to keep lights on and food in the fridge. Therefore, I had little respect for Bonita and Z."

"Where Z at?" I asked.

"We tried to locate him after he disappeared the minute Bonita was shot. No one knew his full name. All we knew was Z."

I became more inquisitive. "Is he my daddy?" Deep down I knew what her response would be.

"Nita, he came around after you were born, so no." Then in an agitated tone, she said, "Be happy that Big Belle raised you. Shit, she yo daddy."

She then went on to say that I favored this dude named Brian from down South. She said that my momma used to sneak in the alley with him when they were in Mississippi visiting Aunt Claire. Aunt Claire was Big Belle's youngest sister. Aunt Margret said that they loved staying with her. She then started lusting about how fine Brian was and how he seemed to like her first. "But, of course, your momma got all the boys," she said in her normal jealous tone. She went on to tell me that when my momma got pregnant with me, it seemed like I was born a couple of months of them finding out. She said that they didn't ask who the daddy was because they could tell it wasn't to be discussed. She said that she was sure there were other men, but my momma died before telling them.

The Moscato had my aunt on a roll. She had told me more than I had heard in years. I knew that momma messed with a boy from down South, but no one said his name. "I can't help but to love the woman that had me, but from what everyone says about her, I'm ashamed. Who am I? Who will I become? Where will I go? My DNA comes from such an undignified woman."

CHAPTER 3

Catalina

"Zonita, grab that other bag for me." I couldn't believe that Baby Cat was really moving out. I knew it would happen one day, but not now. I was too messed up inside. I needed her. Plus it's too spooky on our end of the house. I didn't want to sleep back there by myself. When I was a little kid, Cat used to act like Big Belle's momma was standing in our doorway. Big Belle's momma had been dead since before I was born. "Be Ma don't like dark-skinned kids. She used to pinch them. You better go to sleep before she come get you." I don't think that I believed in ghosts; but Baby Cat always had me spooked with her stories.

As I handed Darian the last box, I attempted one last time to get Cat to change her mind. I had enough tears on my face that you would have thought I was at Big Belle's funeral. Baby Cat just looked at me and said, "Boo, don't cry. I'm only moving fifteen minutes away. You getting grown. You gone need a place to sneak off to. Big Belle not about to let you have a boyfriend. You can come every weekend if you like."

Knowing that she's not being completely honest, I smiled, wiped my tears, sniffed hard, and said, "I guess."

"Big Belle, Cat leaving now," I shouted so she couldn't keep ignoring the fact. Big Belle had been sitting around for days not saying a word to Baby Cat. She totally disagreed with Baby Cat shacking up with Darian. I didn't see nothing wrong with it. Big Belle is so wrapped up in Christianity. What has Jesus done for us? He let my momma die, and Big Belle always prayed. I guess Be Ma was a sinner, so Belle got punished and lost her kid. The Bible ain't nothing but a big riddle. Why wouldn't God have made something that we simple people could understand? He gives us preachers, but they have their own agenda sometimes. They not Jesus, so why should we believe them? I loved church when the music was playing and the people were singing. However, the Bible talk put me to sleep.

"Hello!"

"Hey, Nita, tell Big Belle that I'm coming to get you this weekend." Excited and nervous that she would say no, I hung up the phone and humbly approached Big Belle. "Ma! Baby Cat said that she miss me and want me to come stay with her this weekend." I felt like I was talking to a brick wall. When Big Belle didn't want to hear what you had to say, she turned off her ears. I, being as stubborn as she, repeated myself until her nerves were rattled. A totally frustrated Big Belle said, "I don't care. Go ahead, but remember, a hard head makes a soft ass!" Big Belle was a Christian but could really curse. That's why I cursed so much.

I knew that Big Belle was only trying to scare me out of talking to boys. I often wondered why black people couldn't be more realistic about sex like other cultures. Black people say, "Don't have sex until you are married" while the white people sit down and explain the birds and the bees. They then say, "When you are ready, let's talk about it. I want your first time to be a wonderful experience." That's why the white girl's first time is with her boyfriend, and the black girl's first is with her older cousin's friend or her older cousin. As for me, I never got touched by the cousins. They didn't care for me because I was a tattle-tale. Plus I was determined not to be like my momma. I didn't know if she had done the nasty with cousins, but I didn't put it past her.

"Hey, little girl, I see you've made it." I hate being called little girl, but I guess sexy Darian could call me whatever he wanted. Oh my god, I was totally crushing on Baby Cat's fiancé. Baby Cat told me on the way there that Darian had proposed. I couldn't help but start dreaming about my future. I hoped that I would find a fine man like Darian one day.

"When is the wedding? Can I be in it?" I had so many questions. Baby Cat started laughing. "Now, Nita, we couldn't have picked a date that soon, and of course, you will be in it. You are my sister. I tell you what. We'll talk about it tomorrow when Darian goes to work."

Both Darian and Baby Cat were about to graduate from college. Cat said that she was waiting on a job in her field, which was broadcasting. Darian, on the other hand, was becoming an engineer but decided to take a low-paying job at Lowe's hardware store while he waited. Baby Cat said that Lowe's loved him. "He is so smart, he can tell a man what to buy to build a two-story home without using a computer."

I was so happy for Cat; she seemed to be so in love with Darian. She continued to brag about him. "Girl, my boo even goes to church. Big Belle may forgive us for shacking up if she knew. He wants us to get married at his church, which is fine by me. This church is the bomb. The Vessel. Have you ever heard of a church name like that? Girl, it's so much better than that old-fashioned hymn-singing church we were forced to go to. I wore a pretty dress, and no one pulled it down, nor did I see eyes constantly rolling."

"First, giving honor to God, the pastor, members, visitors, and friends. I am so happy to be in the house of the Lord one more time. The Lord has brought me out of the darkness, and he's continuing to bless me every day." Cat was reminding me of Mrs. Polkey's hypocritical words. "Nita, do you remember that night we caught her and that boy twenty years younger than her making out in her car? I ain't trying to judge, but she the main one that gets up in front of that church and tells the young ladies to act like ladies and wear their skirts longer." I knew just what Cat was talking about.

"Yea, Cat, I know what you mean. She the main one pulling up her skirt, and with little boys at that."

Baby Cat could really let it flow when it came to talking about those church members at First Baptist. She seemed to be scarred by the many wrong acts that she witnessed at that church. There was some good there. Heck, Big Belle could stir up the Holy Ghost. Unfortunately, others caused young folk like Cat to become deaf. She couldn't hear Big Belle or the sermon. I hoped that going to that church would help her grow spiritually.

As for me, I knew the Lord. I had him in me. Everybody used to always tell me that they seen something in me. Big Belle used to tell me that I would be used by God to draw others closer, and if I refused, I would go through many trials. If Big Belle only knew that she was scaring the shit out of me. I knew the Lord, but I thought, Damn, I am a kid. I want to have fun first. When I get old like her, I'll shout around the church too.

Baby Cat and I had been chatting all day. When we got together, we could shut the world off. However, her man would be home soon, so I guess she was done talking. It was time for her housewife duties. "What you cooking, Cat?" I didn't remember Cat cooking anything but oatmeal or microwave popcorn. "Girl, I'm cooking my boo a T-bone steak, Caesar salad, and baked potato." In total shock, I managed to say, "That sounds great." I wondered how she was gone pull this off. I was regretting the fact that I didn't pack some of Big Belle's leftovers.

Baby Cat's feet weren't even touching the floor. She was up in the clouds. "If this is what love feels like, then I can't wait to fall deep." It seems like Cat is always smiling.

"Nita, I am so blessed. I know Big Belle say this is a sin, but I believe that God knows that Darian and I are committed like we are already married. The Bible says that he knows our hearts. So why we gotta sign some papers to be married? I'm tired of praying every night that God forgives us for fornication. Why would he forgive us anyway when we do it again sometimes right after we pray. Then it's praying time again. Darian is a praying man himself so double prayers are going up."

I couldn't believe how serious Baby Cat was acting. I guess that she was changing into a real grownup. She never seemed to worry about sins before. Big Belle's constant nagging about Jesus must have gotten through to her. "Catalina, I'm home!" Darian had the sexiest voice that I had ever heard out of a man's mouth. "Hey, baby! How was your day? Dinner will be ready as soon as you get out the shower." Baby Cat had her shit together. She got the man calling her Catalina. I had forgotten that was her birth name. Well, she'd always be Baby Cat to me just like Big Belle will always be Big Belle.

It felt good to get away for the weekend. I missed Big Belle, but I needed to get out of that old-fashioned lifestyle. I had never stayed with a couple that wasn't married. They were young, in love, and ready to conquer their dreams.

Baby Cat's cooking was pretty good. I had to cook my steak in the microwave however. She scolded me, saying that you supposed to eat expensive steaks while they are still pink. I guess that's why we eat pork, I kept to myself. Darian loved it. He was from the suburbs and has rich parents. His daddy was a doctor, and his momma was a big-time lawyer. They must have been paying the bills. The townhouse that Cat and Darian lived had to cost more than Darian made at Lowe's. I'm sure they didn't mind. Darian was definitely going to make it big someday. Baby Cat said that he even sings. She said he sang "Jesus, You Made Me" at the church, and the roof almost opened and let heaven in the church.

After dinner, Cat and her man decided to feed each other dessert, which left me all alone. I didn't mind because they had all the good channels. There was even a new series on the Urban Channel called *You Didn't Take My Man, I Gave Him to You*. I couldn't stop laughing. This shit was hilarious. The show was about these dumb women that think they have taken some other woman's man. Most of them thought that every man wanted them because they had a home-wrecker booty. That's what one of the silly women said to her man's wife. None of the dumb women ever stopped to think about the fact that they didn't have shit. All the wives were beautiful women; they were smart, and they worked out so their butts weren't a wreck. When the other women met the wives, they saw that these women were very confident. They were definitely not women that would allow anything to be taken from them. My favorite character was Mildred. She was in her forties and was a successful store manager of a big corporation called MK's. She said that she normally didn't stoop to other bitches' level, but she had to let this bitch know, "You didn't take my man, I gave him to you." The ghetto girl, 'cause women don't act like that, switched off, saying, "He loves me. That's why you are a bitter old woman." This show kept me rolling.

I knew that it was getting late, but every time I would doze off, I was awakened by the sounds of high-pitched moans. Since I had never felt a man inside of me, my body was tingling from the noises. My pajama pants were getting very moist, and my patience for my first was getting low.

CHAPTER 4

My Freshman Year

By the end of the summer vacation, I had visited Baby Cat's enough. She wasn't the same anyway. I didn't care too much for the new Cat. She was so fancy that she even expected us to call her Catalina. Darian had become her world, and I found myself consumed with jealousy. I was jealous that Baby Cat had little time for me when he was around, and I was jealous that I didn't have a man like Darian. Therefore, I'd rather stay at home. Anyway, school was about to start back.

I was so nervous about high school. I would be attending Concord High, which was the same high school Baby Cat went to. She was popular and smart, so I hoped that I would get some slack since I was her little sister. I was more unique than Cat. I dressed different than most of the girls around here. Like Cat, they all wore the same brands. These brands had to cost more or they were not popular. I thought that those jeans with the big M on the pocket were ugly, and I didn't care if they cost 350 a pair. I would take the money Big Belle gave me and buy thirty-dollar jeans. I rocked those jeans and loved being the only girl noticed in them. Other poor girls also wore them but made sure that they weren't noticed.

"Nita, are you up?" Big Belle still tried to treat me like I was a little girl. "Yea. I been up." I wasn't lying either; I had been a little nervous about my first day of high school. I had all kinds of things racing through my mind with older boys at the top of the list. "Look at my baby going to high school." I felt a lecture coming. "Nita, I know that you think I'm old, but I've been around the block a few times. Peer pressure is tough in high school, so remember who you are and don't let anyone talk you into messing up your life." I knew that Big Belle was worried that I would be just like my momma. Well, she was wrong. My momma got her ass kicked a few times, let her sisters tell it. As for me, I will never take no whoopings. If I had to knock somebody out, I would do just that.

Homecoming was quickly approaching, and I had made it through the first month of school drama free. I kept to myself and kept my head in my books. I actually made straight As so far. Guess I was as smart as Baby Cat. I couldn't help but hear how all the kids were making a big fuss over homecoming. I didn't think I would enjoy it from what I heard them talking about. The pretty girls bragged about their dates. No boy had said two words to me, much less ask me to go with him to the dance.

The couple of girls that spoke to me asked if I had my outfit ready. "I didn't think about even trying to go, so no."

"You are going with us."

I didn't know these girls like that, but oh well, I guess it was time that I stepped out the box. "I guess I'm going," I said, trying not to sound punked.

Suddenly the stress began. I knew that I had always wanted to be different, but now I felt that maybe I needed to blend in with the hip crowd if I wanted to meet some fly boy. I wanted a guy just like Darian.

"Big Belle, can I have some extra cash, I need an outfit for homecoming. I have to look fly." I was so anxious that I didn't realize that she was asleep. Then I figured I would ask her later. "As a matter of fact, I would wait until I go to Cat's house this weekend and look on the Internet for ideas."

Big Belle was in her sixties, but she acted like she was a hundred and stuck in the dark ages. It was a damn shame that we had no Internet. I didn't even have a cell phone. I wasn't at all surprised that I didn't get much money 'cause the damn light bill was too high. The air conditioner ran nonstop because Jack's diabetic asthma having ass couldn't take the heat. I knew it I had to sacrifice for Big Belle's precious burnt up husband.

Big Belle ended up giving me only enough money to buy a cheap clearance-rack outfit. Having an eye for fashion, I was able to hook myself up for something dirt cheap. Thank goodness our school dressed casual for homecoming dances. I didn't think that I could get a fancy dress for that cheap.

Cassey, Lauren, and I decided to meet for dinner at Rose's Chicken first. As I approached them, I noticed that their laughter was getting louder. "Girl, what you got on?" I had looked myself from head to toe at home, and I thought that I looked great. They had on expensive brand clothes, so I guess they looked better. I was ready to fight they ass and go home when Cassey said, "Girl, don't pay Lauren any attention. I like your style; it's different. I knew she was lying, but it saved them an ass whooping.

"Sexy chocolate, do you wanna dance?" I just turned my head like I know he can't be talking to me. I was the only dark-skinned girl right there but sexy? I've never been called. He wasn't taking no for an answer, so I looked him in the eyes to say no. Once I seen him, my heart started racing, and I couldn't say a word. He was beautiful. "I'm Marcus, and you are?" For at least two minutes there was complete silence. Finally I said, "I'm Zonita." I was a wreck; my knees were buckling as he pulled me by the hand on to the dance floor. He pulled me close, and I was in love. I was impressed that he knew the words to the throwback song by The Fortunes. My aunts and uncles used to play the oldies but goodies every time they visited.

I'D RATHER GO TO HELL THAN THE HEAVEN THAT YOU'RE IN

"Let your love fall on me. You will be my honey. I will catch you, and I'll never let your love hit the ground, for you are the love that I found." He sang so softly in my ear. I was as moist as I was that night at Cat's house.

Feeling very confident, I walked home with my feet off the ground. I was so high up in the clouds that I didn't even realize that those girls left me. I danced with Marcus all night so they probably figured that I was a booty call. After all the stories Baby Cat had told me about her and boys in the backseat of a car, I'd rather walk. I thought I was ready for my first piece, but I was too scared. My knees never stopped shaking from the dance floor to when Marcus kissed me good-bye. He probably thought I was a kid and would never talk to me again. Oh well, at least I had been chosen. Besides, he probably has too many girls. He's a junior, and he plays varsity on the basketball team. He told me that he hopes to be in the pros when he graduates. "Ching Ching." I guess I was a fool not to get up with him on the first night, but Big Belle said that the love of money was the root to all evil. I would never be one of those gold-digging girls.

"What's up, sexy chocolate, I mean Zonita". Oh my god! It's him. I couldn't believe that he remembered my name. I dreamed of Marcus all weekend. "Hey! Marcus," I said, trying to sound as grownup as possible. It must have worked because he popped the big question. "When are we going to hang out?" I knew what that meant 'cause boys like Marcus always looking to score. He must have known what I was thinking since I was hesitant to answer. "We ain't got to do nothing. I just want to enjoy your company. You eat, don't you? I know this fire gyro joint." I could never resist a charmer like him. So trying to sound like Cat when she accepted Darian's many proposals, I said, "Yea, I'm down." He then explained that he would pick me up after basketball practice around sevenish. He was getting sexier by the minute. "OK," I answered while I thought about Big Belle telling me that I couldn't go.

"Big Belle, I'll be sixteen in January, so shouldn't I be allowed to date?" Nawl that would never work to rebuttal Big Belle after she says no no no. "How about I say something like, "Ma, me and my friend going to this new gyro joint for dinner. Everybody gone be there. It's the new hangout spot." I decided to make the lie even better by saying

I'D RATHER GO TO HELL THAN THE HEAVEN THAT YOU'RE IN

that there was a studying area and everything. "They even have computers with free Wi-Fi. I can work on my projects since we don't have Internet." The lie sounded good, and it worked. Before Big Belle could pick up on the lie, I rushed to my room to get ready.

"What should I put on? How should I style my hair?" My brain was flooded with questions. I concluded that if I did something sexy with my hair, I could wear anything. Hair makes a woman in my book. I had one of those faces and head shapes that could wear any hairstyle: short, long, sleek, or big. Since I had a sleek quick weave in, I couldn't do too much. It may loosen, and I would hate to lose a track on my date. So I decided to loosely plait the hair in a few sections. The hair was synthetic, so I could dip the plaits in boiling water.

"Nita, what are you doing with my big pot." Big Belle was so nosey; but I had to be nice, since she was letting me go. "Ma I'm going to dip my plaits in it." I knew what was coming next. "You are just like your momma, always doing something crazy to your hair."

After deciding that I would wear some jeans and a see-through shirt with a tank bra under. I took my plaits down. That was a good decision. My weave looked brand new. The curls were slightly crinkled and the blonde tinge against my dark skin was as pretty as a Reese's Peanut Butter Cup. Maybe he'll call me Reese's tonight. OK, Zonita, get out the mirror before you find something wrong. It's 6:45, and you need to be walking down the block! I had told him not to pick me up in front of the house. I knew that if Big Belle laid eyes on his fine ass, I wouldn't be going anywhere. I would hate to have to dishonor her and die.

After waiting until 7:05, I began to worry. Where is he at? Damn maybe he was early; surely, he would circle back through. Or maybe he's not coming since he knew that he wasn't going to get any. While I was mesmerized in my what ifs, I did not notice him coming down the street. He pulled up, bumping our song and singing loud, "Let your love fall on me." Feeling like I needed another shower because I was nervously sweating while I waited. I cutely said, "Dang, you late." I was too nervous to say anything else.

Marcus never lied; the gyro was super fire. I ate half and decided I would take the rest home to Big Belle. I couldn't eat too much anyway since I was so busy talking to Marcus. As we walked around the park, holding hands, I thought to myself, He's nothing like the jerks that Cat told me about; I could talk to him all night. I was feeling something that I had never felt before. I love my family, but this was different. In a way, it was the first time that I had felt any love toward a man. I cared for my uncles; I couldn't stand Jack, Big Belle's husband, and since I don't have a Daddy, I didn't know how that felt.

"If you gone kiss me good night, do it now, please." Marcus just looked at me like I was some crazy chic. I laughed and said that it was getting late, and he would have to drop me off quickly because Big Belle didn't need to see him. And I wanted him to take his time with that kiss. Big Belle couldn't move too fast, so I figured he would have pulled off, and I would be at the door before she sees him.

CHAPTER 5

My First Piece

A year later, and the love birds were still as happy as ever. Since I had a boyfriend, I had decided to take Cat up on her offer. "Baby Cat, what you and Darian doing this weekend? I was hoping that Marcus and I could hang out over there." Cat didn't seem too quick to welcome us. "Girl, I don't know, Darian and I are real busy planning the wedding. I have to meet with his mother to discuss and make important decisions like what venue we will choose." Since they are, they are footing the bill. I have to make sure that she is in agreement with everything.

Catalina had always been a little narcissistic. Now she had become excessive. When we learned about narcissistic personalities in sociology, I was blown away. The person was described as being excessively preoccupied with issues of power and vanity. In other words, they only care about things that make them look good and feel like they are in control. Everybody around them was pretty much beneath them. The teacher said that there wasn't a cure. Big Belle said the Jesus is always the cure. So if Cat really prayed to God, she will stop being a bitch. Right then, I needed her to be cured.

I was trying to have my first piece that night, so I was determined to convince Catalina to let us use her place.

"Catalina!" I said, trying to sound grownup. "Marcus and I just want to watch TV. You know that Big Belle still ain't got cable."

After promising that we would clean up what we mess up and leave early, Baby Cat finally gave in. "OK. but don't do nothing that I wouldn't do."

"I won't," I said, sounding confused. As I recall, I was her lookout girl on several occasions. Now, just because she was about to get married, she acted like she could do no wrong. I really didn't like this new Catalina. It seemed like she buried Baby Cat.

Well, at least I waited until I was sixteen for this. It was OK, but definitely not like I thought. Marcus didn't moan like Darian, and I didn't scream like Cat. It was over, and we had plenty of time left. Then we decided to sit and talk, but never again looked each other in the eye. We actually sat with our backs to one another. "Did you pray?" I sounded so stupid, and I felt worse. Then like a dummy, he replied, "Pray for what?" I couldn't stand a dumb person. "For forgiveness," I snapped. I hated when someone acted like they didn't know Jesus, so I let him have it. "Don't you know that we not married so what we did was a sin. If you don't repent, then you will go to hell."

I must have turned Marcus completely off because that would be our first and our last time. I was feeling so stupid, and I knew it was all my fault, so I just tried to forget that I ever met Marcus. However, I cried so much that Big Belle thought that my allergies were acting up again. "Nita, what's wrong? Have you taken your allergy pills?" I really didn't care what she believed, so I lied, "Yea!"

For the next month, I walked around the house like a zombie. All I ever did was eat and sleep. School was horrible, and I was thankful that it was almost summer break. My grades had drastically dropped, and I was a total loner.

Marcus was graduating and had been told that he would be drafted into the NBA. He had so many girls surrounding him. I thought that he was different from the other guys; unfortunately, I was wrong. Hit and quit it was what they did, and that was exactly what Marcus had done to me. I wanted to talk to somebody, but Big Belle would just say one of her rhymes, "If you ain't married, then he is a much right man. He has just as much right to be hers as he has to be yours." Then she preached. "That's why you got to let God lead you and wait for him to send you your man." That's exactly why I didn't talk to her.

I wished that Baby Cat could take some time out of her important life to help me. With very little faith that she would answer, I decided to give her a call. "Hey, Cat, this Nita. Can we talk?" I couldn't believe it; she actually said that she would come pick me up and that we would have a late dinner. I was ecstatic, thinking that the ole Cat was back.

When Cat immediately started talking about the wedding dresses, I realized that this was Catalina. I had thought that she was gone listen to my problems, but she only wanted me to see those ugly dresses that we had to wear. "Nita, guess what, you are going to be my maid of honor." Any other time, I would have been happy; but because she could care less about me, I didn't care if she got married or not.

I was so busy feeling sorry for myself that I didn't pay attention to the wedding date. Cat said that they decided to the move the wedding date up. The wedding date was now set for June 30. I couldn't believe that she would be getting married in just two months. Cat went on to explain that the reason for moving up the wedding date was because they had an unexpected surprise. I then became very curious. "What's happened?" Cat's eyes got huge when she told me in an excited pitch, "I'm pregnant." I never thought I would hear those words come out of her mouth. She always said that having a baby would mess up her flawless body, and she refused to live like Big Belle. She said she would have to be well-off before having kids so that she could pay for whatever surgery it took to make her perfect again. Well, Darian had gotten his first job at a big-time company, and they had his parents.

CHAPTER 6

The Wedding

Big Belle seemed to be on cloud nine these days. She has a pep in her step and a smile on her face. I guess she was so happy that Jesus done answered her prayers. She knew that Catalina was pregnant but grateful that she would be married before the prize got here. They all acted like this baby was the first baby ever to be born in to our family. Heck, Big Belle had fifty grandchildren. Some of them were born not by sin. I wonder if she loved them more. Anyway, I'm sick of it.

I couldn't wait until this wedding was over and the little ugly baby was born. I felt like I couldn't stand to hear anymore bragging about Cat. "Nita, you should see the crib Cat and I picked out." There she goes again. Big Belle wasn't even aware that I was paying her no attention as she continued to rattle on about the wedding and that baby.

Since I was maid of honor, I had to help Cat with everything. I wished that she wouldn't have chosen me. I had too many frustrated thoughts: I'll never get to be a bride. I'm so different than her. She fake as hell, and you would think that she grew up around money. She talks proper all the damn time and eat raw steaks. I bet she ain't gone eat no chitterlings at Thanksgiving ever again!" Chitterlings were our favorite. We used to drench them in hot sauce and eat until the whole pot was empty.

I really couldn't stand her, but I did love her, so here it goes. It's time to be fake for the day. "Catalina, are you ready for your big day?" I didn't sound like myself, but her rich soon-to-be mother-in-law was around. Therefore, I couldn't sound too ghetto.

"What if my dress don't fit? I'm fat already, and I have five months left." Oh god, don't tell me Cat is about to be a bridezilla today too. She had been driving everyone crazy for the past two months. I couldn't help but laugh at her when she started crying about her hair. "My hair! Look at it!" She got exactly what she deserved for going to the hairdresser of Darian's mother. It was obvious that Cat didn't have white people hair. I may not have been to beauty school, but I could do some hair. She had done got too high and mighty to ask me. Now she's sitting, looking like a black frizzy-head Cinderella. At least when Brandy played a black Cinderella, she wore braids.

I could never stand to see messed-up hairdos, so I figured that I would have to pull out my bag of tricks. I then told her that after she finished with her makeup, I would hook her up. "K," she mumbled. I guess she ain't so fancy now, knowing that she needed me.

"There's that beautiful smile," Big Belle said as she switched around in her hot momma dress and her high-heeled shoes. Big Belle was hilarious; she moved slow all week, but when she put on her church heels, she could outwalk me. "Thanks to Nita; she always did know how to make me look fly!" At that moment, it felt like Baby Cat was back. It was probably her hormones making her a little crazy, and her nerves were probably bad. We all know that Catalina don't talk like that no more.

It seemed like forever, but finally, it was my turn to walk down the aisle. The maid of honor was the last girl to walk before the flower girls. I had never been in a wedding, and I felt that it was a bunch of crap. Now my nerves were bad. I walked, praying that I wouldn't trip. I was too clumsy for four-inch heels. I must admit that I looked good, and so did Darian.

My mind started to lust as I looked at Darian. Wow, look at that high yellow negro. He as clean as Dick was when Haddie died. That's what Big Belle said about all the good-looking men when they got all dressed up. As I got closer to my spot, I started dreaming that this should be my wedding to Marcus, and that I could be having his baby. I would have to change the song. The country song playing was not a black folk love song. I didn't have nothing against Erin Murray, but I'm gone need some Eddie Gibbons playing. "My Girl, My World" was the song that all black TV shows used for weddings.

When Baby Cat walked through the doors to the aisle, I could do nothing to stop the tears from flowing. She was stunning, from her hair to her princess dress to the glow that surrounded her. Then this beautiful bass voice, sounding like Eddie himself, started singing, "I only need you to make my life complete. The first time I laid eyes on you, I knew that you were the one for me. That day when you became my girl, my world."

Cat had stolen my dream, and I was confused. I didn't know how I felt. I was happy for Cat but consumed with jealously. I was embarrassed of my thoughts. What was wrong with me? I knew the Lord was unpleased. I wanted a blessing, but I refused to bless. As they said their vows, I said a little prayer, "Lord, forgive me for having these hateful thoughts. Father, help me. Give me strength so that I can be loving and be happy for these two as they join in holy matrimony. In Jesus's name, I pray. Amen."

I was immediately filled with joy as we all clapped to welcome Mr. and Mrs. Darian Fowler. I was even happy to see Big Belle and the rest of the family crying tears of joy and relief.

The food at the reception was actually good. My steak was well done. I ate everything on my plate and the rest of Big Belle's. Lately, I had been eating us out of house and home. That is what Big Belle said anyway.

Not long after we ate, I heard Aunt Margret yelling, "Is that my song?"

I'D RATHER GO TO HELL THAN THE HEAVEN THAT YOU'RE IN

"Oh Lord, these white folks' gone have a fit." The DJ had found the Wobble. She then embarrassed me when she told me to come wobble my big butt with my Tete. I like her nerves, but my butt ain't big. I should leave her big ass out there off beat. She was lucky that I was prayed up, so I decided to go ahead and turn the party up.

"Hey, big girl, back it up," I sang as I jiggled on to the floor. The DJ must have liked my jiggle because he played the Wobble so many times that we were back in our seats and the white lady with too much to drink stayed on the floor. She had caught on a little bit, so she thought she was throwing down. She kept saying "Hey, big girl" over and over again. She was about a hundred pounds, soaking wet, so I hoped she didn't make any of the big girls that she kept walking up to slap her. We had some ghetto folks in our family that love to fight. It was a good thing for her that they usually fought each other.

It was starting to get late, and I was starting to get sleepy. For some reason, I had been going to bed earlier than usual. To top it all off, the drunk lady was coming my way. I know she is not about to bother me again, I thought. Several people had kept stopping her before she got to me because they knew that I also liked to fight. There wasn't no stopping this lady; she got all up in my personal space and shouted, "What's up, sexy girl? Let's dance." I was about to snap on her when my jaws started to water, and I ended up rushing to the restroom. I puked up all that food until I was weak and starving all over again.

Finally the night came to an end. Darian and Cat left two hours ago. They said that they were going to rest before catching their flight in the morning. I don't know how much rest they would get; maybe on the plane. Cat said they were going to Jamaica. I bet Cat wished that she still smoked. I heard that's all the Jamaica people did.

On the way home, the car smelt horrible. Big Belle had packed all those damn plates to take home for Jack. I had to smell the stinky shit all the way home. Then she had the nerve to tell me not to forget the plates when we finally made it home. I knew she was bringing them home to Jack, so I should have dropped them on accident. It ain't nobody's fault that he was too old and ugly to go to the wedding.

CHAPTER 7

Out of Wedlock

Sunday, he preached about unconditional love. "Jesus didn't have no respect for persons. He loves us all." Amens filled the church. However, these same people amen him no matter what he says. Every now and then Rev. Lipe's sermon was straight from the Bible and understandable; but as for his opinion on any other topic, I managed to tune him out.

    Maybe I was a little harsh on Rev. Lipe, but he had a reputation. During his reign as the minister of First Baptist, he has been rumored of doing some pretty bad things. Mrs. Lipe is the second Mrs. Lipe since he's been the minister. I wasn't trying to judge, but how you gone get up and tell young folks what not to do, and you cheated on the first wife with your second. Gossip is that the current wife went from secretary of the church to the first lady in no time. Rev. Lipe got off easy since the first Mrs. Lipe died of cancer. The word is that the slut he is with now pushed her in her grave and kicked the dirt in her face.

"The doors of the church are open. If you don't know Jesus, here's your chance." I knew Jesus, but I eased on up there for prayer. I may not have believed in Rev. Lipe's opinion, but I believed in the power of prayer. As I was asked to give a statement, I did my usual. My face filled with tears and my nose started running. "I need somebody to pray for me. I keep doing wrong over and over again. I'm asking the church to pray that God strengthens me."

I should have asked them to pray the constant sickness from my body. I had been sick for months now. I thought that it could be karma for teasing Jack. Now I probably had diabetes. Big Belle said that when Jack don't eat, he gets sick and when he eats the wrong stuff, he's still sick. All I knew was that something had to give. I hadn't been disobedient, well not that much, so I hoped that my days weren't shortened. Uggh! This Bible stuff got me crazy. All I do is wrong. If I die, I'll probably go to hell!

Although I had been sick a lot, I wasn't losing any weight. I wore dresses and leggings all summer, which hid the fact that my butt was gigantic. This was apparent as I tried putting on a pair of jeans that wouldn't come pass my thighs. My junior year of school was starting, and I would look like a hippo. "I could always call Baby Cat and get the recipe for one her many diets that she went on every time she gained a pound."

Sitting around the house was all I had done lately. School started back, but I came straight home every day and went to sleep. Lauren and Cassey always came over, begging me to hang out. They were always going to the gyro place. The last time I went there, I got sick from smelling the food and from missing Marcus. Aside from the sickness, I also didn't want to be around people because of feeling so ugly. "Zonita, you lame," they complained.

I didn't go anywhere, and I also wasn't about to be involved in any school activities. I had always thought about cheerleading since it was a boy magnet sport, but after gaining so much weight, I would look inappropriate in one of those tiny skirts. My butt had gotten out of control. The boys said that it was sexy, but I felt that they were just making fun of me. I didn't get too depressed over not going out for cheerleading since I had never been a girly girl anyway. I could play basketball, but my energy level wasn't high enough for any sport like that. I figured that I would finish high school doing as little as possible to get by.

I'll never forget the day when I came dragging in from school with my usual hateful attitude, and Big Belle told me to sit down for a minute. Furious about her stopping my daily nap, I said, "What?" After noticing the serious look on Big Belle's face, I became humble. "What you need, Ma?"

"Nita, I think you need to see a doctor. Have you been with a boy yet?" Fine time to ask, I thought to myself. Then I lied, "Nawl. I ain't done that yet." Big Belle obviously knew that I was lying because she insisted that it was time for me to go see the gynecologist. Oh no! I was scared as hell of going to the coochie doctor.

Baby Cat had told me all about the very painful experience of going to the gynecologist. She said that a piece of meat felt better than a piece of steel. "Girl, they put this cold steel thing up your coochie and pop you wide open so they can see if a baby in you." That was the very reason that I was never going to have sex. However, the fear of the doctor went away when that boy touched me. Marcus was my first, and I was thinking that he would most likely be my last. Sex wasn't all that it had been hyped up to be.

As I sat in the cold room and stared at the scary warnings on the wall, I became extremely nervous. "One time was all it took" is what one of the signs said. This sign also has a picture of a young girl with a big belly. The poor girl didn't look to be any older than I was. I was completely grossed out as I stared at the other picture. It consisted of a young teenage boy with a tongue full of blisters. This brought back memories of Cat talking about the ugly dude named Dudley from down the street. Cat vividly described Dudley's tongue to be full of blisters, and that his lips were a crusted over gray color. She specifically told me to never kiss a boy with a mouth like that.

I shouldn't have ever kissed anyone. Sex was definitely highly overrated. I did it one time. Now there I was, waiting in a lonely room for

Lord knows how long, waiting for the results. I didn't see any blisters on Marcus's mouth, so hopefully, I don't have blisters; and we used a condom, so I can't be pregnant. By the time I started worrying about even more serious malfunctions, such as AIDS and hepatitis, in walked the doctor with Big Belle. Big Belle sat down looking like I was already dead. I was preparing myself for the "year to live" speech when the calm doctor said, "You are pregnant." After explaining that he would give us some time to talk, he just walked out and left me in the hell like room with a furious-looking Big Belle.

Speechless about the news that I just heard, I sat and stared at a heartbroken Big Belle. I began to sob as I noticed that her eyes were closed and that there was a wrinkle on her head. I knew that she was busy praying to Jesus. I hoped that she was asking Jesus to stop her from killing me. While my prayer was for the doctor to come tell me that this baby was dead. I knew that I sounded cruel, but I was devastated. I wanted to be different than my momma. I was going to do as Big Belle say. Love, marriage then babies. The only problem was she didn't explain what to do between the lust and love part. I knew that Big Belle had kids, but the way she would shut down any sexual conversation made me wonder if she ever had sex. I couldn't even imagine her getting busy with grandpa or Jack.

It was official. After two minutes of hell, I was pregnant. Cat said it felt like heaven to her, but I missed out on that feeling. God had me confused. Why did Cat have sex unmarried several times and get spared of hell? I done it once, and it felt horrible plus I'm having a fatherless child.

Overwhelmed with books and pills, I just sat on my bed and cried, "I ain't no different than my momma. I'm sixteen and pregnant, which was even younger than she was with me." I don't even have a boyfriend. Marcus was famous already. He had gotten a contract and everything. I knew that he was probably going to be mad. A baby would be the last thing that he needed in his high-profile life. I wasn't even thinking about the fact that I was going to get paid. I was too busy wrapping my brain around the fact that I was having this baby alone. Suddenly, I became angry, thinking about the idiots that would call me a gold digger. Pregnant or not, if I heard one person saying bad things about me, I would be fighting.

"Nita, we need to talk." I already knew what Big Belle wanted; it was only a matter of time before she asked who the daddy of this baby. Feeling angry, I thought about saying, "Mama's baby, pape's maybe." I wondered if she would like a taste of her own medicine. But humbly, I told her that I guessed that it was Marcus's; he was the only one I said with total confidence. At least I did know who the daddy was unlike my mother.

After I got over the shock of being pregnant, I figured that I should let Marcus know. However, I didn't have a way of getting in touch with him. He cut all ties with me when he got famous. Although I wasn't ready to face the drama, I began to question people around school about how to get in contact with Marcus. I wasn't at all surprised as the expected rumors circulated like a gossip magazine. I was pissed immediately as I heard one of the nasty rumors going around, was "Zonita, pregnant and trying to blame it on Marcus knowing that she was screwing the whole football team. She just want that money, being that he in the pros and all." I wished that one person who said these lies would step forward but no it was always he said she said. Anyway they all gone look stupid when he gets his DNA results.

I had been so angry during this pregnancy that I felt like skipping school every day. I didn't care if I passed. Hell, I didn't care if I lived another day. The devil had consumed my mind. It was easy for him to get in since I had become angry with Jesus. I prayed, but he still let this horrible thing happen to me. He exposed me and let everyone know my sin. So I became weak and decided to let the devil win.

Big Belle was so old-fashioned that she wouldn't let me go to church. She didn't want her holier-than-thou church folks looking down on her for letting her teenager get pregnant. I wondered if she did the same thing to my momma. I found myself getting mad at Big Belle. If she had let momma go to church, maybe she would have lived her life differently and may still be alive, I thought. Since she had me at a young age, she might not have been so judgmental and allowed me to go to church with her, or at least, she would have had a conversation with me. Hell, Big Belle didn't have much to say to me at all. She stayed on one end of the house, and I stayed on the other. I missed laughing and talking to Big Belle, but it was for the best. I may have not wanted the baby, but if I had to have it, then I didn't want it to be ugly; and Big Belle had said that if someone gets on your nerves while you are pregnant, then your baby may come out looking like them. I remember Big Belle talking about the reason her baby son held his tongue out all the time. She said that this ugly man named Mr. Wanky thought he was so fine that he held his tongue out as all the women walked pass. She said that while she was pregnant with Uncle Ralph, she cursed old Mr. Wanky out on a regular. Uncle Ralph was born with his tongue out, and it's been like that ever since.

Big Belle acted like I would be giving the baby away of something, which at times, didn't seem like such a bad idea. She never mentioned it becoming a part of our lives or that it would even make it into this world. Maybe she hypocritically prayed it to death too. I didn't know or care exactly what her problem was. I had decided that I couldn't hide forever from the good church folks; a baby was coming sooner or later. I was going to church the next Sunday whether she liked it or not. What she gone do? Put me out? I would have been perfectly fine with that. I figured I could always go stay with Cat.

With all the emotions flooding my thoughts, I had forgotten that Cat and I were pregnant at the same time. If we were real sisters and closer in age, it may have been an exciting thing. Unfortunately, there was the married a well-to-do family and having a baby, then there's the hot little girl Zonita who couldn't keep her legs closed. I could imagine them talking, and I didn't blame them. There was Cat, pregnant with a husband and a perfect life, and there I was with nothing but a baby taking my life.

Maybe a good church service would be good for my heart and soul. I could tell that Big Belle was ashamed but relieved that at five months, I could camouflage my belly with a bag dress, which was trendy and very classy. My butt was getting bigger by the day, but I just looked like I had a coke bottle shape.

As church went on, all I thought about was going up for prayer, and since Big Belle would have a heart attack, I wouldn't say anything about being pregnant. I quickly planned to mention that I needed prayer for a crisis, which would be a big part of the truth.

I felt so much better after church service and the soulful prayer from the mothers of the church. I knew that God was in control and that the devil was beneath me. That was until Sister Polkey came flying up to our car. "Belle, when is the great grand baby due?" I was heated; her nosey ass was always in somebodies business. Big Belle sat speechless. I guess she didn't want to lie while on holy ground. A nose like Mrs. Polkey could always smell trouble, so she got her answer when Big Belle didn't answer. Big Belle was rolling her eyes faster than I was mine, which let Mrs. Polkey know that she had struck a nerve. She floated off like she had hit the lottery. Gossip meant more to her than money. It seemed to be as equally gratifying. I really didn't care what she thought she knew. Her old ass ain't Jesus, and therefore, she or no one else has a heaven or hell to put me in.

CHAPTER 8

The Tragedy

Catalina didn't say much about me being pregnant and being due a few months later than her. They said that I was due on March 10, and she due on January 1. She was always bragging about having her baby on New Year's and getting all kinds of special gifts. "What else could the royal baby need. Her rich white mother-in-law done bought the whole store." I hated feeling so much jealousy for Cat and her baby. Every now and then, she would say, "Nita, you can have this. I don't want my baby in that."

Baby Cat and I were both having boys. I hoped that they would be close, but I doubt it. My son will be born out of wedlock. Many will treat him like he is not as good and that will mainly be our family members. In our family, if your baby is a bastard, you don't get a baby shower. People just came after the baby was born to drop off sympathy gifts. Catalina and Darian looked so happy at their baby's shower. It was more like a baby storm. There was enough stuff for several babies. She had a replica of everything. I was envious, but at least I would get all the stuff that she didn't want.

Everybody had a joyous time chatting with the happy couple. I wasn't happy. I was tired of hearing about that baby. Black people get on my nerves thinking that a baby gone be cute because the momma is light-skinned and the daddy extra light with wavy hair. That's one more reason why my baby would be mistreated. Marcus was not as dark as I was, but we would surely have a darker-skinned baby. Neither one of us had the "good hair," so our baby's hair would be nappy.

Catalina had everything going for herself. Darian was moving up quickly at his job, and she was moving up in the church. She said that she spoke at a woman's day program. Her topic was about virtuous woman. She said that everyone praised the way she spoke. Now every time you turned around, she was speaking at different programs at different churches

Big Belle went from being disappointed that Cat was shacking up to being ecstatic in her renewed life. Big Belle always wanted her kids to know the Lord. To have one as an up-and-coming minister made her extremely proud. The look on her face was loving and satisfied. It was much different than the look she often gave me. Catalina had always loved being the center of attention. "Isn't that how ministers start off? They talk well and people listen, so their calling is to preach." Catalina has always been good at telling people what to do, so I wasn't surprised that she would be appointed to lead the flock. In a sweet, proper, but stern voice, Catalina would say, "The Bible says!" Then her lashes flutter, and everyone looks. Now she could draw them in with her seductive way with words.

"God is my rock, my sword, and my shield. He is a will in the middle of a will. I know that he will never, I said never, let me down." Catalina spoke this old hymn song that Big Belle used to sing with such clarity and proper wording. I couldn't help but laugh, and I believe that Big Belle even giggled.

The many people that filled the pews of "the vessel" just shouted calmly, "Glory be to God." They were so proper that they sounded like they were saying got instead of God.

I couldn't take these people; I'd rather be at First Baptist where the real Holy Ghost is at. The people were rich though. When the offering came about, people actually spoke of things such as, "I would like to donate twenty thousand to this wonderful establishment." Catalina was getting paid well for speaking to a bunch of rich people who thought their money would get them to heaven. Big Belle's hymns that she used were kind of interesting; but the rest of her sermon had too many complicated, big words. Big Belle was up there saying amen, knowing that she didn't understand a word.

I was glad when it was time to go. We did our part by coming and supporting Catalina who was too high to see us. We had to sit down low because we didn't have big donations. If you sat low, you were obviously closer to hell than the rich who sat high. Big Belle said that Jesus has no respect of person, but I couldn't tell. Church is run through Jesus and the ones with lots of money are run better. They can take thousands and pay a doctor to heal a member's cancer while at the little poor church, if a member gets cancer, they pray then they sing and shout six months later to the song "In the Upper Room."

Catalina was showing well. She was about eight months by this time. As for me, my butt just kept getting larger. Big Belle said that the same thing happened to her when she carried her boys. Catalina was slender with a little basketball belly. She carried her baby boy totally different from Big Belle. At least, I had beaten her at something. She didn't know how to carry a boy baby.

"Lord, help me if I would have known something so tragic would happen. I would not have thought those bad thoughts about her baby. I cried and prayed as we sat at the hospital, watching the devastated parents mourn the loss of their baby."

Catalina had three weeks left and seemed to be OK when she fell down the stairs of their townhouse. She instantly went into labor. But because something happened to the baby during the fall, he didn't survive.

"Here I am, not wanting this baby in me, and she loses hers. God, what are you doing?" I cried. Big Belle was so weak; she looked like she had aged ten years in ten minutes. She wasn't praying or nothing. She, the strongest person in our family, and I felt that she was broken right then. I felt so sorry for her but even more sorry for Darian. He stood with his nose pressed against the window, staring at his dead baby. Darian Jr. was as beautiful as I had imagined. I knew that I had been jealous, but I never wanted my aunt Catalina's baby to die. Deep down inside, I felt that it was all my fault.

Catalina never cried about the baby. She just became more religious and stern. She preached to us, "God don't make no mistakes." People came from all around to hear Catalina's testimony. She said that God was trying to get her attention, and that he has great works for her to do. Sounds like what Big Belle said was going to happen to me. I wondered if she had told Cat the same thing.

I didn't spend time at Catalina's like Big Belle did. I was about to have this baby, and I didn't want to upset her. In a way, I was glad because Big Belle said, "Cat ain't the same anymore." She worried that Cat was going to push everyone close to her away. She said and I couldn't believe that this came from Big Belle's mouth, "All she cared about is that church."

Darian rarely came to our side of town, so when he came, I figured it was important. After I overheard him telling Big Belle about his and Cat's problems, I decided to eavesdrop even harder. He told Big Belle that Catalina wouldn't touch him nor talk to him. He said that he had suggested counseling, but she refused by saying, "Jesus is my counselor." Darian was wondering if Big Belle could talk to her and let her know that her husband was suffering. Big Belle may have been old, but she wasn't dumb. She knew that meant that Baby Cat wasn't pleasing her man. Big Belle will tell you that she listens to her old music because she hasn't always been saved. One of her favorite songs was "No Pain, No Gain," and her favorite line of that song was "Be a momma to the kids and you know what in the sheets."

Darian said that Cat never wanted to do any of the things that they used to do. I had always been envious of them. They were always traveling to romantic places. They had the perfect love life, and Cat bragged to me on numerous occasions on how gifted Darian was in bedroom activities. To think that she doesn't want it now made me think that she needed a Jesus-appointed psychiatrist. God said be fruitful and multiply. I guess since her baby died, she didn't plan on having anymore. Well, she obviously didn't plan on having her husband either. He was over there, crying and shaking and shit like he was going through some kind of Catalina withdrawal.

    I couldn't help but watch his fine ass leave. "I'm sitting here wishing I had a man like him, and she pushing him away." As Darian pulled off, I noticed that he stopped at the block. The boy handed him something. I guess he need some weed. Cat said that they used to get high when they were younger, but they quit so that they could get good jobs. Darian had been so stressed out, he may smoke something stronger. I hoped not. He was too fine to be a crackhead.

CHAPTER 9

Jack

I was so glad that the teachers came to me so that I didn't have to go to school. Since Big Belle finally had Internet, they used e-mail most of the time. I was happy to be passing all my classes. I had done well in school as long as I wasn't dealing with those fake kids. Teenage pregnancy wasn't a big deal these days, but I still never managed to deal with the constant put-downs, especially the ones that involved the name Marcus.

Any day now I would be having this baby. Marcus said that he wasn't denying the baby but needed a paternity test as soon as the baby was born. Marcus, you are the daddy; so Marcus Jr. and I would be just fine. I figured that I could at least pretend that I was having a baby by a daddy that wanted him so my boy would be a junior, Marcus Junior it is.

This baby was coming so fast, and I was becoming so scared. "What if I'm a horrible mother? I'm too young! How can I do this alone?" My days were consumed with darkness as I waited for the pain and misery that everyone talked about. My worst pain was not having the daddy around. I needed someone to seem interested in this child's birth.

One day, as I went to the kitchen to refill my Kool-Aid, Jack kindly asked me to go to him. He began to tell me that he knew that I didn't like him very much. He said that he didn't blame me either. He went on to explain the reason why he became a bitter ole man. He said that he loved my grandma with all his heart but hated that she allowed the children to think he was a good-for-nothing man.

"I told Belle that your momma was gone get killed if she didn't stop, and when it happened, she blamed me like I had prayed for her death." Jack was as serious as I had ever seen him. He then went on to tell me that my momma, Bonita, wasn't as bad as the family made her out to be. When he got with Big Belle, my momma was fifteen. She was the oldest girl but by far the nicest. "Yes, your momma seemed wild. She was beautiful like a grown woman by the time she was sixteen. The older men around thought she was grown, and many tried getting with her." Jack explained how he tried to protect momma, and that he told Big Belle about the things he heard on the streets. He said Big Belle looked at him with such hatred that he decided to keep his mouth shut. He said that he wasn't surprised when my momma started sneaking out of the house.

Jack went on and on about momma. He told me that she smoked weed but that the rumors of other drugs were most likely lies. He then talked about how he became a nobody to our family. He said that he had plenty of money when he got with Big Belle. I always figured that, I thought. He had been injured working in the coal mines in which he worked for years. Before getting with Big Belle, he said that my grandpa Rufus died and left a shitload of bills. "When I got with Belle, she was a poor good-looking woman with nine children," he said in a convincing tone. The youngest kid was Cat; she was seven. He said that his money helped a lot but ran out quickly when Big Belle's oldest son, Uncle Jimmy, got into trouble with the law. "He was dealing to do drugs," said a frustrated Jack. Jack couldn't watch Belle suffer, so he let her pay a big shot lawyer. All his money was gone in a year to keep my Uncle Jimmy from doing thirty years. Jack said in a spiteful tone that yes Uncle Jimmy got off, but as I know, he's now doing life.

Jack could have kept his money. After listening to his story, I could understand why he was so mean. He gave his last to help a deadbeat like my uncle only to be hated when his well ran dry. Jack said that none of the kids had respect for him after he got broke but my momma. "Big Belle once told me that Bonita meant beautiful in Spanish. That was a good name for your mamma; she was beautiful inside and out. She may have made some bad choices, but she also made plenty of good ones." The story then gets emotional. "I remember when you were born, your momma was so proud of little Hershey's Kisses. The family tried to make her feel bad about having you out of wedlock, but they didn't affect her. She used to say, 'I may be nothing but a nothing ass stripper to ya'll, but my baby gone have the world.' He said that momma refused to be on welfare, and that she had so much pride. He said that she would fix my hair and dress me up like I belonged on the *Cosby Show*.

I couldn't believe that Jack had me laughing about my momma. Heck, I couldn't believe Jack had me laughing period. I didn't even smell any weed. I guess Jack was trying to help me feel better about myself. He did just that; I felt amazing. To know that my momma loved me, rather she wanted to have me or not, gave me inspiration to love my baby boy.

I slept like a baby that night, which was unusual these days, since the baby had my body deformed. I must have been in a deep sleep because I didn't hear any of the commotion going on. By the time I made it into the living room, Big Belle and Sister Polkey were sitting on the couch, crying about something. "What's wrong?" I asked but was scared of the response. "Jack passed away some time this morning, Nita." Big Belle sat quietly while Mrs. Polkey answered my questions. I guess Big Belle knew that none of us liked Jack, so she figured that I would care less to know that he had left this world.

I was blown away by this news. Heck, I had just started liking Jack. Who would have thought that my first real conversation with him would be my last. It didn't even seem spooky in the house. I always thought that if Jack or Big Belle died that I wasn't staying there. I didn't want them to haunt me like Be Ma did Baby Cat and me. It was actually peaceful. Jack must have known that he was leaving and decided to share the little love he had left with me. God is always trying to show me something. "Well, God, I don't want to see it yet. Let me live my life first. Wait until I get old!" I prayed.

I was surprised that most of Big Belle's family showed up for Jack's funeral since he wasn't liked very much. Jack obviously didn't have much family. I didn't remember hearing one word about them. There were no blood relatives of his at his funeral. That's when it hit me, We are his family. Too bad it was too late to tell him. At least my momma showed him some love when she was alive. I then began to wonder if they would see each other in glory. "I believe they will because although they may have chosen hell when they were here. I believe they chose heaven before leaving."

Jack's funeral was going quicker than any other funeral I'd ever been to. The choir sang an upbeat song as if no one was sad that Jack was gone. I'm sad, so I'm gone say something, ran through my mind over and over again. Next thing I knew, I was at the front of the church. "How many of you really knew Jack? That's ironic 'cause that's all he ever wanted. Since he didn't get it, he became someone who kept to himself. Before Jack died, I had the privilege of really getting to know him. In one night, I found out how caring he was. He was a man that gave his last to help others and never rubbed it in their faces, which is what God told us to do." When I said that, Big Belle began to scream. I guess that I had struck a nerve. So instead of causing more guilt, I closed by saying, "I'm thankful to Jack for caring enough to help me."

Lately, I had been emotionless, but Jack's death brought me to tears. I was so hurt that he died after sharing his deeply kept feelings with me. I also wished that he would be able to see my baby boy, but I guess he had done what God needed for him to do, so his time here was up.

CHAPTER 10

Marcus Jr.

I couldn't believe that March had arrived so quickly. Although I was still very nervous about having this baby, I had decided that I had better start preparing for him. As I folded the last bunch of baby clothes, I realized that I had more than enough for this baby. Baby Cat had given me all her extras. I didn't ask what she did with all of Darian Jr.'s stuff. She tried not to show it, but I know she's in a lot of pain. I am also hoping that she would work things out with her mind and have another baby soon.

Preparing for my baby became extremely difficult when I had to stop every few minutes to go to the bathroom. I started to take some containers into the bathroom with me, but after the last trip, there was no need because my pee didn't stop. I figured it was my water breaking, so I calmly gathered my things and told Big Belle to call the ambulance. Big Belle could drive pretty well, but she was also pretty slow, and I believed I needed to hurry. The pains were like mild period cramps but were happening every few minutes.

By the time I arrived at the hospital, I was in nonstop pain. I felt like I had been constipated for months and was about to get some relief. Of course, there was no going to a bathroom. I was transferred to a bed with lights brightly shining between my thighs. Still feeling the need to use it, I followed the doctor's instructions and pushed hard. One long but hard push, and out he came, yelling at the top of his lungs. "My god, how big is that boy?" said an excited Big Belle. I couldn't even tell that she was mad at me; she just looked at my baby and smiled.

Marcus Jr. was 9 lbs. 5 oz. and 23 inches long. He had caramel skin just like his daddy. Who would have thought that I would be so in love. When I looked at him, I saw a reason to live. I saw a reason to make something of myself. If no one else ever loved me, his would be enough.

"I can't wait for your daddy to see you." I hadn't seen Marcus in nine months. I heard that he was injured and wouldn't play for the remainder of the season. Every now and then, my friends would tell me of the gossip that circulated around school. They said that Marcus had supposedly been asking people if I had the baby yet. "Guess he'll be coming around soon to get his unnecessary test." I knew what Big Belle meant when she said mama's baby, papes maybe. It didn't mean that you don't know who the father is, it meant that the baby would always have a mamma but a daddy sometimes.

Even though I knew that it wasn't cool to trap a guy with a baby, deep down I hoped that Marcus would look at his twin, fall instantly in love with him, and then fall in love with me. I started dreaming that Marcus and I would get married and go to church with our heads held just as high as the old folks.

I thought that I was over Marcus, but the thought of seeing him again had me so optimistic. I wanted us to be a family. I had one more year of school left, but Marcus made enough money that I would be able to drop out, get my GED, and go to a cosmetology school. I had gotten even better at whipping hair.

"Nita, you have company," yelled Big Belle. I had been home from the hospital for one day, and no one came to see me. Since I wasn't married, the church folks didn't come, and everyone else must have thought the baby and I were irrelevant to the world. My mind was torn between dreams and reality as Marcus stood outside my door and asked to come in with the same sexual chocolate voice. The baby screamed as soon as he heard his daddy's voice. "Thank you, Jesus!" They had father-son chemistry; he had to love him now. If he didn't, he would after the results were in. Marcus you are the daddy, I thought and chuckled to myself as I had all pregnancy long.

I was in shock when Marcus asked to hold Marcus Jr. The cutest tear rolled down his cheek as he cradled his baby tightly in his long sexy arms. He was so emotional that he apologized and everything. I didn't care about him abandoning me; I just wanted him right then and there.

My dreams of us being a family were quickly shattered as he began to explain himself. "I will always take care of my son." Oh my god! I am not trying to hear what he is about to say! He then, with a little hesitation, tells me that he is madly in love with a wonderful woman that he planned to marry and have his own family with. At that moment, I became an ignorant, self-righteous, "you can't see yo baby" baby mamma.

Marcus had found out that his injury would be a career ender. I knew that would take away from my income, but it was about more than the money. Maybe he wouldn't be so popular, and that model bitch would leave him. She ain't nothing but a gold digger, and I bet she will never have kids 'cause she'll die if she get a stretchmark, I thought. I was most definitely venting and had become bitter that my body was destroyed. I loved my baby but how was I supposed to get a husband with a rippled stomach caused by another man.

All of a sudden, Marcus Jr. wasn't so cute. He looked like his nappy-head daddy. I was hurt, so I couldn't help but feel that way. It seemed like my life was full of bad choices. I couldn't get nothing right. Big Belle says to turn it over to Jesus, He'll work it out. But I wonder what he done worked out for her? Look at Catalina; she can't do nothing but praise these days, and her baby is dead. So at this point in my life, I doubted that Jesus stuff.

I used to believe that prayer worked. Now I didn't know what to believe. I had been praying all night for this baby to shut up, but he was still crying. "I've changed his pamper, I've fed him," I shouted to Big Belle who had eased her way into my room. Normally, I would have an attitude about her telling me how to raise my baby, but I was at the end of my rope. I wished that she would just take him so that I could have some peace. Without saying a word, Big Belle took the baby from the crib and placed him on her breast and rocked him. Big Belle must have had some type of magic titties 'cause the little black boy went to sleep.

Thank you, Jesus! I guess prayer does work. Well, maybe for Big Belle. She believed in the power, and for then, so did I.

CHAPTER 11

My Senior Year

Marcus Jr. was a six-month-old healthy baby and had only been to the doctor for shots. Every time he thought about getting sick, Big Belle gave him some of the roots that Aunt Claire sent her from the country. I know that Big Belle and them were Christians, but the root stuff reminded me of voodoo. Big Belle had a lot of stories to tell about the old ladies from down South. Mrs. Gussy was her favorite to talk about. She said that she was so afraid of Mrs. Gussy but always visited her candy store with all the other kids. "The kids used to say that she had eyes in the back of her head." I could tell that Big Belle really believed to this day that they were telling the truth. Supposedly, one of the kids used to try and steal candy all the time until one day, Mrs. Gussy told them that she had seen Pookie took the candy, which piece, how many, and she even knew when he swallowed it. Big Belle's eyes still got big when she told how Mrs. Gussy would chant "The boy gone pay."

Now what was really messed up about Mrs. Gussy was that she was the praying healer of their village. Big Belle said that every time she got really ill along with the others in her town, she was taken to this spooky room in the back of Mrs. Gussy's candy store. She said that there would be a big pot boiling all the time with smoke filling the room and chants of Mrs. Gussy. This story always reminded me of some fictitious Halloween story; but Big Belle swore to it and said that she was scared as hell but was always healed.

I almost snapped the first time I seen Big Belle pour something out of a whiskey bottle into my baby's milk. Whenever I would ask what it was, she would call it something that was not in the English language. I didn't ask too many times because, when I did, she would go on for hours how the world is *weaker and wiser* yet dumb as hell. I would get tired of her stories about healing without a doctor as long as you believed in Jesus, but I shut up since I hated to hear my baby cry. "Go ahead, Big Belle, work your magic."

I wanted to share Big Belle's baby-saving tricks with the other teenage girls in my Parents Too Soon class, but most of them were so slow they may tell the counselor who would call DCFS. The Department of Children and Family Services had become a young mother's greatest nightmare. Some of the counselors in our class were dirty. They wanted us to lose our babies so some unfortunate, no-baby-having couple could adopt them. Most of the time, it was a black baby given to a white couple. "I know that times have changed; but I have a problem with this."

"Look at her little locks." That's what DeeDee said the white lady who has her little girl always say. DeeDee is one of the girls in our group; she had a little incident where she had to defend herself against several girls who tried to jump her. Somebody called the police. and she was arrested. Since her junkie parents didn't go get her, she spent the night in jail. Meanwhile, DCFS took her baby from day care when she didn't show up.

After getting out of jail, DeeDee tried getting her baby but was told that her house was unfit, so they placed the baby with a foster parent until she would get herself situated. She said that she visited her baby twice a week but left devastated after every visit. When she asked to comb Prenae's hair, the lady said, "No, she cries when you touch it. Anyway, her locks are gorgeous." DeeDee was afraid that her baby was gone have real dreadlocks if she didn't get her back soon. DeeDee was so sad that she smoked weed all day long. It didn't seem like she would ever get her baby back, and the counselors didn't care. They figured her baby would be one less on welfare if it got adopted.

I didn't get welfare 'cause I got child support and mommy support. I had decided to attend the class anyway because it got me out of regular school. Three days a week, I got out two hours early to attend this class. I enjoyed being around people who felt like me. Yes, I was getting money from my baby daddy, but I was still a frustrated teenager with a baby. If it hadn't been for Big Belle, I probably would have shook my little boy a couple of times and prayed that he shut up.

The videos that they showed us would have opened anyone's eyes. The girls on the videos would snap out. They would be feeding and caring for their baby then, when their cell phone rang, they would ignore the baby. What was really messed up was when the baby interrupted their conversation by crying. They used inhumane measures to shut them up. I felt like jumping through the video and beating them up when it hit me, everybody didn't have a Big Belle.

I still didn't care for school very much, but I enjoyed being the thickest senior at this high school. Besides my friends in the group, I only dealt with a couple of other females. Lauren and Cassey fell out over some boy. I never really cared for Lauren; she thought that her little knock-kneed ass was hitting on something. Cassey and I, on the other hand, were still cool. "Girl, Lauren acted a fool over Jay." I had heard that Jay was supposedly hitting both Cassey and Lauren. "She mad 'cause we are a couple, and she can't have him." I knew that poor Cassey was a fool 'cause all boys are dogs, but at least she was nice and cute. I didn't know why anyone would want Lauren. She was ugly as that thang. I had been waiting for her to say something to me 'cause I wanted to fight her. She had always called herself picking on me 'cause I was poor. I was getting plenty money now but still wearing Levis.

The word was that Lauren was dating some other dude now, so I figured she would stay far away. She knew that once he fixated his eyes on all this thickness, it would be a wrap. Having a baby had filled my body out. Most of the time, I loved the attention. What I didn't like was that everyone assumed that I was fast because I had a baby and I looked seductive. There were times that I wore a long blond weave at the bottom of my back, which made me look so sexy. The insecure boys would say, "Why you wear all that weave?" while the fine boys would just adore me.

I was a brick house and proud of it even if it brought more drama to my life. Of course, my mouth brought even more. I couldn't help but use one of Big Belle's rhymes to shut down the staring of the skinny chicks. They were pretty girls but so insecure of me. "I'm a big fat woman with meat shaking on my bones and every time I shake, a skinny bitch gone lose her home." I was the only one laughing. The others weren't used to old-school raps. Sometimes I felt like I was the only teenager in the world who had a Big Belle. "Maybe I should write a book with all her sayings so the young can get some knowledge."

"Zonita, don't mess with nobody less they mess with her." Big Belle's voice was like music to my ears. If anyone had my back, it was her. She was so right. I didn't start the fight, I just finished it. There I was sitting in the principal office facing suspension and possible jail time, the cameras showed the three girls jumping me; but when the ambulance had to escort they asses to the ER, all the blame was placed on me.

The school psychiatrist was so slow. "Zonita! Why are you so angry? Why do you feel like being so violent?"

"Bitch was I supposed to cradle in a ball and let those three weak-ass girls kick me in the head?" My mind raced and my soul became angered as I listened to this dumb lady for hours.

The crazy people doctor had made me crazy. I then decided to cooperate since I had made it so far in school. I wanted my diploma that I deserved. Plus I thought that I just might go to college and make something of myself.

Marcus Jr.'s money was about to run out. Marcus Sr. was about broke from gambling and whores. He didn't invest in nothing but women with bad market value. In a way, I was glad that he was broke; maybe we could finally be a family. The gold diggers would be done with him as soon as they got his last dollar.

"Zonita Labelle Walker!" I walked across the stage and proudly snatched my diploma. I could hardly believe that I was graduating. I had loss faith a long time ago and didn't see too far into my future. It felt good to have reached a milestone in my life. I guess I even felt like I had a chance to be somebody. I just might make the people out, who thought that I would be just like my momma, out of liars.

After the processional, we all bragged about being grown and done with school. I was shocked when I saw Baby Cat and Darian standing in the lobby, holding a huge balloon that said congratulations. I wanted to be happy but instead I felt numb. Catalina had become so uppity that I rarely seen her nor did I know her anymore. Therefore, it didn't surprise me when she started in on me. " Zonita, what are you going to do with your life?" I guess she meant well, but I took it as she was really saying, "Are you going to go to college so that you can be more than another girl on welfare?" Catalina had a way of talking and looking down on people. She could say something simple that would make someone give up on the life. She was supposed to be working for Jesus, but I thought that if you worked for him, then you should have some nice qualities.

"Cat, you and Darian are coming by the house for the graduation dinner, right?" Damn! Why did Big Belle have to go and do some crazy shit like that? I was not in the mood to get stared at and treated bad when I put on my hoochie momma outfit.

I had made plans to step out. It would be my first time getting to go to the new club that everybody had been bragging about. They said that the music and the men were off the chain. The only bad thing would be wearing the underage bracelet that wouldn't allow me to buy alcohol. Anyway, I planned on getting blowed before getting to the club.

I had started smoking weed earlier that year. The majority of the girls in the Parents Too Soon group smoked. We used our free time to get high. This was the times when the leaders of the group babysit our kids so that we could do what young teenage girl do, party! We did just that only we added a little loud into the equation. Most of the girls sold their link to buy weed. I didn't get link, and I wasn't spending my money on weed, so I smoked off of them. Besides, I was doing all their hair for free.

Dinner was great. Big Belle had fixed all my favorites. Chitterlings in the summer tasted just as well as they did in the winter. Big Belle's potato salad was also good. She said that she learned to make it from Aunt Claire's Belizian friend named Roni. She said that the first time Roni fixed it she thought, "What the heck! This ain't potato salad. Who puts peas and carrots in potato salad?" I'm glad she liked it enough to learn how to make it because I loved it. Big Belle even made a batch of tomato dumplings along with some collard greens and my favorite dessert, pecan pie with French vanilla ice cream on top.

Marcus Jr. wasn't quite two but was definitely terrible. Catalina had made one too many comments about my baby, and I was about to snap. I wasn't a little girl anymore, and I didn't take ass whoopings. Plus I had my own money, so I could do and say whatever I pleased, meaning that Catalina better watch her proper mouth.

"Don't ya'll discipline that little boy? He's going to be hell on wheels when he grows up." OK, I had enough. Just because this bitch's baby died, she wants to act like my baby can do no right. Without thinking, I blurted out some hateful, unforgiving words. "Where your baby at, Cat? Maybe if you weren't such a bitch, God would have let your little white ass baby live." I didn't just stop there either; my mouth kept pouring negativity. "If you knew how to be a woman and please your husband, you may have been pregnant again by now." I felt like pure shit, especially when Baby Cat ran out the room in tears. Darian didn't even go after her. He just sat there looking like she deserved that whooping of words.

Big Belle ain't never been able to do nothing with Cat. So she just sat and called on her Jesus. "Call him up, call him up! Tell him what you want, and while you're at it, tell him that I want Catalina to stay the hell away from me." Well, I knew enough about Jesus to know that he wasn't about to answer my prayers. He answers the prayers of the righteous, and right now, I can't wait to go out and be unrighteous.

I'D RATHER GO TO HELL THAN THE HEAVEN THAT YOU'RE IN

The club and a big fat blunt was calling my name. Maybe if I would have smoked, I wouldn't have snapped on Cat. I understood why Jack chose to be high all the time. It's probably the same reason my momma stayed high. Cat used to stay high herself before she got so holy. I wondered if Big Belle used to get high. I couldn't imagine her doing anything but praising God. For me, right now, being high felt as close to heaven as I would ever get.

I thought I would never get Marcus Jr. to sleep. Big Belle only agreed to watch him if he was in bed. She said that she would never watch him for me to go serve the devil. If shaking my dump truck and getting wasted was serving the devil then I chose Lucifer tonight. You are only fine and young once.

Sometimes I got so mad at Big Belle because she acts like she has never been young. Then I get saddened when I remember that she was just scared that I'm gone to turn out like my momma and get killed. All that praying to Jesus, but at times, her faith was as weak as mine.

After putting the baby in Big Belle's bed, I hurried back to my room to get dressed. All I had left to do was slip on my jumper and heels. Big Belle's eyes would pop out of her head if she would have seen the way my ass looked in my white, sheer short jumper. I danced in the mirror while looking at my butt to make sure it jumped back and forth while staying sexy. I was fly in all angles. "Thank you God and Bonita for this banging body."

Sneaking by Big Belle's room was fairly easy. She probably wasn't asleep but decided she wouldn't preach that night. Maybe she had realized that her preaching made her children chose the wrong things more than the right ones. If she said that I look like a stripper, I may go be a stripper. Hopefully, she's getting the picture and stay in her place. "Shut up and pray; somebody gotta keep getting our prayers through the main line." The weed had me tripping already. I was laughing as I cursed at my Big Belle in my mind.

I was dreading picking up those slow bitches. They take all night trying to get pretty as me, and they always fail. I became crunk as hell when they arrived to my car in less than ten minutes. "Ya'll look cute," I said, knowing that they wouldn't return the compliment. Maybe because I was not cute. I was finer than that thang. So to hell with them telling me; I knew it.

Our stomachs were sucked in and our butts were poked out as we did the fresh girls stroll around the club. Club Bypass was everything that it had been talked up to be. The music was bumping, and every now and then, they slowed it up and played a smoothing cut from the '90s that made me feel like grinding. Of course it didn't work like that. Nowadays, the guys stand on the wall while the girl does stripper moves on his private. I couldn't see myself doing all that grinding for free. Heck, I might as well go cross the water if I'm gone do all that.

There were some fine men up in this club. "Who is that fine sexy dude over there?" DeeDee was always throwing herself on somebody, so I figured I better get in front of her so if he was that fine, he would see all this first. "Nita." How in the hell did this fine dude know me. It was so dark that I had to get closer to see that the fine dude was Marcus whom was as beautiful as ever.

Marcus wasn't alone. He was with this skinny white girl whose nose was so pointy that she looked like she was pointing up at him at all times. He then turned to her after checking me out for all of two minutes and introduced me as his baby mamma. The bitch then began to look me up and down as if I wasn't nothing. She stood there looking like a he-she. The bitch was as tall as Marcus. "It's amazing how a little money could change a person's life."

As the eyes kept rolling and the conversation was demeaning me, I felt the devil tap me on the shoulder and say "Punch her." By this time, Marcus, absent daddy ass, was asking me why was I at the club with a baby at home. Before I knew it, a slew of words came out my mouth and ended with one of Big Belle's lines "I'm two times nine, and I ain't got nobody to mind."

This would be our first and last time in Club Bypass. The bouncers tossed us out like we were a bunch of thugs. Oh well, from what I heard, it was well worth it. They said I laid that bitch out. Last thing I remembered was her pulling Marcus by the arm and calling me a ghetto booty heifer. I obviously blanked out because, when I came to myself, the white girl was black and blue, and I was being carried out by an oversized male. My girls were talking so much crap that they were thrown out also. Besides, they rode with me, so they better have had my back.

We all carried our heels in our hands as we walked a mile back to the parking lot. "Dang, Nita, why you have to get so angry? You should have just ignored them. I thought I was gone get me one of those rich fine men." That's all DeeDee ever thought about, a piece of ass. She already had two kids with no future of getting off of welfare. "Girl, there will be other clubs," I said, trying to shut her up.

We were all blowed when we arrived at the club; now we were sober and in need of a blunt. As we were approaching the car, a dude in an old Cadillac sitting high off the ground, stops beside us. "Hey, you in the white, come here"! That would be me; I was the only one in white. "Nita, come on, girl, you don't know him; he could be a rapist." Candace was a hater. She rarely ever talked, but now her homely looking ass wanted to rain on my parade. "Last time I checked, that car is mine." Because the night had been a total mess, I decided not to curse her out "Girls, I'll be there in a minute." A fine dude brought out the sweet side of me that easily.

Before I knew it, thirty minutes had passed. and I was still standing on the driver's side of Caleb's car. Caleb was his name, and he was sexy as hell. I was in a trance and ready to do whatever. All I could think about was how I didn't know anything about this feeling when I was with Marcus. Since I was older, I had hot sex on my brain. I felt that I could forget the fact that it was a stupid sin.

Oh my god all I could think about was getting all over this boy. I only know his name and that he was twenty-one. He said he was single, so he could be mine. Caleb was definitely my type. I could have stood there frozen in time and talked to him for eternity.

It looked like I would be spending my night with this boy as he trailed me to drop off my girls. Completely out of my mind, I agreed to park my car at Dee Dee's and ride with him. His car was nice. It was a white Cadillac with an aqua top, and his seats were light grey leather. The sound system was so loud that I had to shout to talk so decided to shut up. Anyway, after one hit of the blunt that he rolled, I felt like we were flying in the sky. Instead of riding on 24s, I felt like we were on 64s. I don't think that they make rims that tall, but I was tripping hard.

It seemed like we had driven for hours but got nowhere. I couldn't remember where he said he lived and if he said where he lived. I didn't even know if I asked. At this time, I recall an uncomfortable feeling took over my body. My mind functioned very slowly while by body felt like I was racing someone. I wanted to say something, but my mouth wouldn't move. The music and the drugs had my mind gone.

I was so thankful when the car finally stopped. Caleb was a gentleman; he held my hand, which was great since I could barely walk, and led me through this dark building. We walked up at least twenty flights of stairs. Well, maybe not, but I felt like it was equal with the moon.

As soon as the door shut, Caleb had my clothes off. He must have had taken them down while we were climbing the stairs. I don't know what came over me, but I was all his. He kissed, licked, and blew me away. My toes were curled up like I had on shoes that were three sizes too small. This must be heaven 'cause hell can't feel this good, I thought. I was completely consumed with the lust for this man. He was grown and sexy, and I wanted every part of him over and over again.

As the sun shined on my face, my mind began to race and I wondered, Where am I? Everything came back to me as Caleb came walking back into the room. He was fully dressed, and I was fully naked. I felt cold and lonely. I was also feeling very depressed as I thought about how angry Big Belle must be with me.

I became full of anxiety as I imagined how bad my baby was being, and how Big Belle would kill me for sure if she knew how much I had served Lucifer. I kind of remembered what I had done. I did know that some or all of it felt pretty good. I knew for a fact that I didn't pray. My mind was as far away from Jesus as it could get.

I guess I didn't do anything too stupid since Caleb's little fine self just sat down beside me and started kissing me all over again, which shut down my prayer attempt. "No stop," I cried. I have to get home. "To your baby," replied a concerned Caleb. I hadn't mentioned my baby to Caleb so his reaction caught me off guard. "How do you know about Marcus Jr."? He explained himself by telling me that he knew I had a baby because only grown women possess a body like mine. He said that I had a different kind of thickness in the hips. Caleb was fine and charming. I just laughed, thinking, It's these stretch marks on my stomach, duh!"

Caleb's green-eyed, caramel-skinned ass could look at me all day. However, if I didn't get home, he may be looking at me in my casket. I knew that if I wanted to see this boy again, I was going to need a babysitter. She would never keep him for me to date or party, so I would have to deceive her into thinking I was doing someone's hair and really be going to see my boo.

Knowing that I couldn't just pop up at home, I decided that I would call Big Belle first. My cell phone had no service, so I asked Caleb if I could use his. He was reluctant at first. I guess he cared for me already because he deleted something. I figured it was another woman's picture. It didn't faze me; I was confident that his other bitches were history. Anyway I had more important things to think about like my conversation with Big Belle. "What lie could I come up with"? "Hello" said an anxious and irritated Big Belle. "This is Nita. I'm all right. I tried calling you, and you didn't pick up. Belle, there was a road block by my girlfriend's house, and the officer said that I couldn't drive with my license plate light out or I would get a ticket. I didn't want to raise your insurance, so I slept here at Dee Dee's. I have to drop off this job application first, so I'll be home in an hour or so." These were some awesome lies. Big Belle didn't know anything about caller ID, so she didn't know if I called or not, and she don't know anything about my car. Since I didn't have a clue where I was, I couldn't say I was on my way from Dee Dee's.

Big Belle was super quiet on the phone. She was most likely praying the whole time so that she didn't start back cursing and let me have one of her good old-fashioned lashing of words. I wasn't worried about her; all I had was Caleb on the brain. It only took him twenty minutes to drop me off at my car, which was ten minutes from home. I drove home slowly since I had some time and some lie to burn. I daydreamed about the boy that had rocked my world—Mr. Caleb Mosley. I always thought that I liked tall guys, but Caleb was only 5 ft. 8 and 160 pounds at the most. However, his little body was cut up. He looked like he lived in the gym. His haircut was a nice, clean bald fade. Although this look was sexy, he looked better in his old picture on the dresser where he had dreads that hung past his shoulders. Oh well, he don't need hair. He would probably make me do it for him.

    I dreamt all the way home that this man was the man in my life. I didn't even know what he done for a living. When I asked, he responded, "I gets money." I did know that he had a car, his own crib; and he is fine, so he can be mine.

CHAPTER 12

Father, Help Me

A few years had gone by, and I was approaching the grown age of twenty-one. Marcus Jr. was almost four and was a big boy that went to school. He stayed at school all day, and I lay with Caleb all day. I wanted a job so that I could start back getting my child support, but since I was forced to get on welfare a year ago, Marcus is now paying welfare instead of me.

I had thought about going to beauty school, but I wasn't sure if I wanted to make a career of doing hair. Dealing with black women and their hair could be too much for me to handle. I hated the fact that they were so afraid to get their hair nipped. A haircut was completely out of the question. The fact that our hair don't live as long as other cultures was a fact that most black women ignored. I found myself explaining the dead hair fact too many times. Therefore, I just didn't know if I could hold my cursing tongue long enough to please these insecure women.

I had some regular customers that paid me well. However, I chose to smoke up most of my profit. The rest of the money was given to big baller Caleb who begged on a regular. He promised that he would double my money. I gave up on expecting it to be doubled. I would have settled for it singled. After years of waiting, I never saw one red cent.

I had been with Caleb for almost three years now, and I was still confused about our relationship. I felt that we were a couple. We spent our days and most nights together. However, there was something missing. Yes, he was a beast in the bedroom, but he was not husband material. I may not have been wifey material either, but I intended to get my life together. Caleb, on the other hand, acted like he had no desire to change. I had a feeling that he would be fighting pit bulls and selling dope when he's old, and he still gone be broke.

I couldn't believe that I was still with this boy. After our first six months together, I started staying overnight for weeks at a time. Sometimes Marcus Jr. and I were there alone while he went on his weekend runs. I have never seen any benefits of Caleb's runs, but he was always so cocky when he got back as if he had conquered the world. Every now and then, he would buy me an outfit and a pair of shoes. He managed to keep the baby in Jordans, so he thought he was being such a good man. At times I wanted to scream, "Where is my fucking money?"

This boy always driving my car on his runs 'cause his is a gas guzzler. Most of the time, his car sat and looked pretty with those big rims. He would go sit in it every day and get high, but it rarely started. Watching him as he bragged to his friends about how much his shit cost made me want to throw up.

I was so disgusted with Caleb as he lied about how much money he had but wasn't even paying for his apartment. I almost crawled under a rock when I found out that the project apartment was in his ex-girlfriend's name. She supposedly owed him so much money that she let him keep her apartment and said that she is staying there. That was the reason why he could pay his bills. "Hell, who couldn't pay a hundred dollars a month?" Since I had been with him, I had paid most of it, and I was pretty sure that before me, some other dummy was paying them.

At times, I wondered if I even loved Caleb. I loved him while he was going down on me, but when he came up, the love vanished. I repeatedly told myself that I was going to end this mess of a relationship. However, his little fine ass had a way of sucking me back in. "You know you are my boo" worked for Caleb every time, especially when we were high. He smoked blunts for breakfast, lunch, and dinner. I smoked while my bad ass son was at school and again when he went to bed. I couldn't deal with my son while I was high.

Caleb often bragged that weed made him smarter. I didn't feel very smart. I did feel that it helped life pass by quicker. Three years of my life had passed, and I felt that everything that happened was a total blank. I didn't even remember the last time that I had prayed. I guess getting high every day had me so high up that I didn't have a need to pray.

I hadn't been home in so long that I felt like a visitor. The old house had started to feel creepy, and it had a staled smell. "Big Bell, what you cook?" I asked, trying to start up a conversation. Big Belle and I weren't close anymore. She had become so disappointed in me. She didn't just come out and say it, but I could hear it in her voice and see it all over her face. "I didn't cook anything. There's nobody here but me, so Mrs. Polkey brings me a plate most evenings." It broke my heart to hear big Belle say this. She had always loved cooking her own food.

The aroma of the fried chicken was gone, and you could smell the age of the house. Big Belle had been in this house for a lot of years cooking, singing, and praying. Now she's stop cooking. Soon she will stop singing and praying. Then there would be no house or a Big Belle.

It felt good being home for a change. I decided to go in the kitchen and cook in hopes that the comforting feel would return. "So how is church?" I knew that if nothing else worked, church would get Big Belle talking. "Church is good. God is good, and we could never praise him enough. I am so glad that Jesus loved the world so much that he died for us." Big Belle was about to start shouting at home, which was fine with me. I needed some Jesus in my life.

It was times like these when I started to believe again. I knew that I had been sinning and not even caring about it, but Big Belle says Jesus will forgive me if I asked. This battle of good and evil thought that I had was driving me insane. It was crazy how one minute I was convinced that Big Belle was right about Jesus and then my mind flips to the fact that Big Belle was old and I was scared of getting old. When you're old, you have no choice but to believe that you have lived right enough to go to glory. As for me, I'm scared of heaven and hell.

After hours of cooking, I had managed to get the house smelling like usual. "How them greens taste?" I asked with great pride. Big Belle chuckled and said, "Their eyes may roll, teeth may grit, but none of these good ole greens they gone get." I laughed so hard that I cried. You would have thought that I had not heard that rhyme a hundred times. Knowing that Big Belle liked my greens had me feeling that I had learned something. I may be going down the wrong path, but if I learned anything from Big Belle, it would be the fact that anybody could turn their life around. I felt like I was a lot like Big Belle, so it wasn't a surprise that I would have learned from her over time. I always said that if I get old, I would be just like her. I would be beating the church door down and praising the Lord all the time just like her.

Strictly kidding with my mind, I thought, Hell, I may even become a preacher. Catalina was a preacher just because she spoke well. I knew that I would have to be a totally different type of preacher than her. I would be real so that the young folks don't feel like I felt. Sometimes the people in church are so holy that they push unbelievers farther away.

I personally believe that God wants us to smile rather than frown when spreading his word—the word that shall set us free of our jailed minds. Preachers like Catalina are so into themselves and their own beliefs that they can't become humble and stop youngsters like myself from wanting to go in the opposite direction from them.

Big Belle said that Cat rarely visited or called. Who could be so into church and preaching their messages but couldn't show love to their own momma. "The Bible says that charity begins at home, and in order to preach to others, you must have your house in order" was one of Rev. Lipe's many sermons.

Feeling my usual rage about holier-than-thou folks, I ignored Big Belle as she tried showing me a magazine. After she shouted at me to snap me out of my evilness, she handed me a magazine with Baby Cat on the cover. Catalina wasn't quite thirty but looked forty on this picture. I guess the Vessel made her believe that she had to be dressed down to look like a woman of God. Her dress looked like some kind of new nun's outfit. Cat always had a nice shape, but you definitely couldn't tell now.

Big Belle explained that Catalina's church had a monthly magazine that would feature some of Catalina's sermons every month. I quickly flipped through the pages as if I cared. I definitely didn't want to hear no Jesus talk coming from such a cold-hearted woman that Catalina had become. "Unconditional Love" was the title of Catalina's article. "I got to read this." How could someone who shows no love preach about it? After reading the first two sentences, full of words that required a dictionary. I tossed the magazine back on the table.

"Mommy, yo phone ringing," Marcus Jr. was always playing with my phone. The little boy had gotten too grown for words. There were three missed calls and seven text messages, all from Caleb. "Bitch, I know you out with some other nigga." Obviously, he had been calling me and texting me all evening. For some reason, Caleb had become so insecure that he wouldn't believe me if I told him the truth. It wasn't like he was taking care of me, so after reading his final text in which he threatened that he was going to see his ex, I decided to ignore the rest of his calls. I was so pissed that I felt I may never reply.

Just as the baby and I were about to lay it down, I heard a gentle knock on the door. When I looked out the window and saw Caleb's car, I hurried to the door before he woke Big Belle. She didn't believe in no man coming to her house that late, no matter how many babies you have.

Caleb was such a thug. He came to Big Belle's smelling like a blunt factory. He also kept that pistol on his side at all times. I knew that Big Belle would have a fit as soon as she laid eyes on him, so I hushed him and pulled him pass Big Belle's room and back to mine.

As soon as we were in my room, he grabbed me by my neck and began to scold me. I could have sworn that I didn't have a daddy, so why did he have his hands on me? "Come on, we're going back to my place." My first option was to curse his ass out, but I knew that he was too high and crazy. Plus if Big Belle heard him, it would have been a shootout. I done the only thing that I could, I got the baby, and we went with Caleb.

What had I gotten myself in to? Caleb cursed me the entire way. He didn't allow me to drive myself knowing that I would have tricked him and disappeared or go to the police. After calling me every name that described fat and ugly, he let me know that he was going to beat the shit out of me when we got to his place.

I had always been pretty tough in fights, but my opponents were always girls. Caleb was scaring me. He was full of evil spirits. He really didn't have a reason to hurt me, but being that he was temporarily demonic, I decided to swallow my pride and plead my case. "Boo, I only spent time with my grandma because she was lonely." I couldn't get my sentence out well before he cursed me. "Bitch, if you were with her the entire time, you would have answered your damn phone"!

Caleb was completely crazy and was not going to listen to reason. I was tired of explaining myself so I it looked like I would be fighting a dude. What was worse than the beating would be my baby watching it. I didn't want him growing up and becoming a woman beater. He was asleep, so I figured if I laid him down in the room then let Caleb hit me with no retaliation, the fight would be over quickly, and the baby wouldn't wake up.

Caleb stormed in the building before me, which was great. I figured he would go straight to the bathroom, and I would have time to lay the baby down. After laying Marcus down, I decided to lie on the couch and act like nothing was wrong. I was not prepared for this type of life, so I prayed, "Lord, what do I do?" He must have answered me because I began to pray. About half way through the Lord's Prayer, Caleb came out of the bathroom. I hurried up and finished my prayer, "In Jesus name. Amen." I guess the time that I had spent with Big Belle helped me realize that I couldn't make it without Jesus. I was thankful that I wasn't high. My brain was functioning enough to give me the wisdom to pray.

Caleb's eyes were larger than usual, which meant that he was no longer high. He sat down on the floor and pulled me to him by my neck. He was choking me, but it felt good. He started kissing me from head to toe. For some reason, I felt like I was falling in love with him again. He apologized for being insecure, and we held each other and had wonderful after-sex conversation. He even said that he wanted me to be his baby momma. What about marriage? I thought? However, I knew that Caleb would never propose or get married. Thug life was all he knew.

My dreams were cut short with a familiar knock on the door. I wondered what Caleb's home boy Zatron wanted at this time of night. I'm sure it's the usual, to smoke a blunt or talk about how many bitches he has run through. Normally he does this in front of me, but this night, he asks Caleb to step outside. Next thing I knew, Caleb was telling me that he had to handle some business.

My heart began to pound as I watched Caleb grab this case that had a fancy gun in it. He had told me that he would never use it. It was Zatron's daddy's gun, and that it was powerful enough to wipe out a lot of people at one time. He said that Zatron's daddy gave it to Zatron when he went to prison. Caleb ended up buying it from Zatron when he was broke and needed some work.

Thank god that Marcus Jr. was out of school for spring break since we were basically stranded. It was the following afternoon, and Caleb still hadn't returned nor answered his phone. I must have loved Caleb because I was worried sick, thinking, I hope my boo ain't in no trouble. That damn Zatron done got his ass into some mess that my baby has to handle.

I was used to being at Caleb's alone but not like this. I had a weird feeling, and I needed to know what was going on. I didn't care for Caleb's side of town, so I never ventured out. From the car to his house then back to the car was the most exposure that I had gotten. Since Caleb had been gone so long, I decided to walk around in search of gossip.

I held Marcus Jr. by the hand and walked toward the park. I had never visited the local park because there seemed to be sounds of gunshots whenever Caleb drove by to holler at one of his boys. Caleb didn't advise that we went there either. He said that a kid was gunned down while playing on the swings less than a year ago.

As I got closer to the park, this dried-up-looking boy says, "Ain't you Caleb's ole lady?" I didn't answer; I just walked faster. The boy was determined to talk to me and blurted out that everyone been talking about how they got them niggas on the South side last night.

I didn't ask that dude any questions. What he said was enough for me to hurry back to the apartment. After arriving at the apartment, I did the only thing that I could think of and called Big Belle. After calling her several times, I realized that she must not be home. I was so used to Big Belle being home when I needed her, especially on a Monday night. Where could she be? I concluded that she must have been visiting late with Mrs. Polkey. Maybe there was some good church gossip that kept her later than usual.

I felt defeated. I needed to get to Big Belle so that she could pray for Caleb. Although I was starting, God had answered my prayers by not letting Caleb fight me. I wasn't feeling strong enough to pray. I almost felt that I deserved something bad to happen since I had been sinning repeatedly. I was too nervous to take a chance on a sinner's prayer. I needed a prayer warrior to pray that my boo makes it through.

I couldn't believe what I was about to do, but it was getting late, and Big Belle hadn't answered. "Hey, Nita, are you OK?" Darian must have picked up on the nervousness of my voice. Trying not to alarm him, I replied, "Yea, I'm good. Is Catalina home?" Darian explained that Catalina was out of the country with some mission group. After letting out some of his frustration about her never being at home, he finally asked if I needed something. I then briefly let him know a little of the truth, and a little was all it took. He was eager to come to my rescue. "I'll be there soon." I knew he would do just as he promised because he was a good man.

For the next twenty minutes, I stared at the window. Shortly after sitting down, I saw the lights of Darian's BMW. I hurriedly grabbed

Marcus Jr., and we went to the car. On our way home to Big Belle's, he asked me to fill him in. Darian sounded like my daddy, asking all those questions. I really didn't feel comfortable telling him how I met this thuggish boy and let him take control of my mind, body, and soul. Thankfully, he understood and told me that I could talk about it when I was ready. He didn't say one more word the rest of the way home.

As soon as I walked in the house, I noticed Big Belle lying on the bed, sound asleep. She didn't budge as we kept up plenty of noise, going pass her bedroom at that time of night. I hated to disturb her, but I was desperate for her prayers. "Big Belle, wake up! I need you." She just lay there with her eyes closed and with a smile on her face. She said, "Child Jesus already know what you going through, and you must believe that the battle is already won." She then went back to sleep.

Feeling like a weight had been lifted off of me, I went to my room after seeing that Darian and Marcus Jr. had fallen asleep on the couch. I was full of glory, knowing that everything was going to be all right. As I lay in bed, I sang all of Big Belle's favorite old hymns. "Jesus is on the main line. Tell him what you want." I sang at the top of my lungs, and for the first time, I believed that he heard my cry.

After sleeping all night and half the morning away, I woke up to laughter in the kitchen. When I made it to the kitchen, Big Belle, Darian, and Marcus Jr. were all eating breakfast. "Good morning, sleepyhead," said a cheerful Big Belle. As I began to fix my plate, I noticed that there was an extra plate that had been eaten. Before I could ask who had joined us at breakfast, Darian smiled and said, "That was Caleb's plate. He is outside, smoking a cigarette."

I was relieved but instantly angered. "Where has this nigga been?" He had me worried all night; however, before rushing out and cursing him, I thanked and praised God. Wow, Big Belle was right. She knew that God had handled my problems without a doubt in her mind. I wondered how a person could have so much faith. I may never know, but I was thankful that she had it.

Caleb was so beautiful, standing there smoking that cigarette, and all I could do was wrap my arms around him and kiss my man. He hugged me and said that he was sorry, but that I would understand if I knew the circumstances. At that moment, as I lusted at the veins popping from his little muscular arms, I would have believed anything that came out of his mouth. I was so in love and ready to show him.

After hearing all about Caleb's gangster activities, I didn't want for any of us to stay in the ghetto. I couldn't believe that I didn't have to lie to get Big Belle to agree to let Caleb move in with us. All I told her was that he was in danger staying there, which was the truth.

Everything seemed to be working out for me. My baby was becoming a big boy. Caleb and I were getting closer, and I knew we would get married as soon as he got a real job. Finally, Big Belle and I had gotten close again. On Sunday, we all went to church, which was Big Belle's only stipulation of us living with her.

"Caleb, wake up!" I was so embarrassed. This was my boyfriend's first time at church, and he falls asleep as soon as Mrs. Polkey started her solo. She did take too long between the precious and the lord. When she got to take my hand, Caleb was knocked out. He already stuck out like a sore thumb. He was dressed like he stepped out of a boys-in-the-hood movie. The Lord says to come as you are even if he was asleep. My mind should have been on the service, but instead, I sat there thinking that I should pretend to have the Holy Ghost and slap him in the face. Then I thought about him waking up and swinging back at me. The thought of everyone thinking that we were in the spirit because of Mrs. Polkey's solo had me dying.

Nobody could stir up the spirit like Big Belle. She had gotten quite a bit slower, and it had been sometime since I had seen her really jump around and praise God. This Sunday, she sat over there on the mother's bench, rocking from side to side. I loved to hear her soulful voice moan. You could feel the message of her song piercing through your soul. "Put your time in. Payday is coming after a while." I loved the song, but I wasn't ready for my payday. I wasn't ready to live right, so I hoped that I had a long while.

Rev. Lipe's sermon was almost finished when Caleb wakes up to the squealing sound of thank ya. It was good to see Big Belle running around the church. It made me think about all my blessings, and I felt like running with her. However, I don't feel the spirit enough to be looking crazy. Big Belle's wig all crooked and her hat that was pinned to her wig is somewhere in the back of the church along with her high-heeled shoes.

I have always feared the Holy Ghost, but I'm glad that it's present. It's a miracle when the spirit of God moves through people. When I was a kid, I used to ask Big Belle what it felt like. She always said that she felt happy. I would laugh and say, "You look just like the folks on *The Price Is Right* that wins a lot of money."

It was time for me to get back into the service. Rev. Lipe would soon be opening the doors of the church. I was going up to rededicate myself to the Lord. I had already been baptized but felt nothing back then. Well, I did feel like I was drowning when the preacher dunked me in the pool. I remember following the other kids up to the front of the church at the yearly church revival. We believed the preacher when he said that we needed to come to the altar so that we may get saved from the devil.

With tears streaming down my face, I cried out, "Father, help me," as Rev. Lipe prayed for my poor lost soul. After praying, he told me that God is a loving and forgiving God. I felt the spirit of the Lord inside of me, and I was determined to spread this good news to as many people as I could. When I finally opened my eyes, I noticed that Caleb and Marcus Jr. were gone from their seats. It kind of pissed me off because I needed Caleb to hear the prayer and think about getting his life together.

Full of hope and feeling like a warrior, I decided that I would sign up for school first thing Monday morning. Caleb surprised me and said that he was going with me and see if college had something to offer him. He then mentioned that he used to twist his own dreads and even dreaded and braided other guy's hair when he was locked up. I couldn't believe that this thuggish boy was considering cosmetology school along with me. I tried to tell Caleb in a nice way that he didn't fit the look of a hairdresser. Most male hairdressers were usually on the sweet side. Caleb just laughed at me and assured me that he was all man. "I guess it was better than a career in an illegal pharmacy."

After leaving the campus, Caleb decided that he needed to stop at his place and gather some of his things. As he slowly gathered his belongings, I decided to read the cosmetology brochures that I had received from the admissions office. Normally, I would feel defeated, but everything was working out. It looked like I would actually be able to do this. Although I wasn't too fond of Caleb being a beautician, I was glad that we would have a chance of getting closer while in school together.

The zero tolerance to fighting did have me a little worried. "Caleb is so fine, and all those females gone be on him." I hoped I didn't have to put a bitch in her place; however with my temper, I just may blank out. "Maybe he shouldn't go to beauty school. I'll try talking him into auto mechanics. I like hard hands and dirty-bodied muscular men anyway."

I thought Caleb would never finish getting his things, but finally, we were on our way. I was so excited to get home and tell Big Belle my news. I knew that she would be proud of me. I was also proud that I would be able to please her. My mood quickly changed as Caleb snapped at me for driving too fast. I knew that I couldn't afford another ticket, so I was pissed as the asshole cop pulled me over.

Caleb was sweating and rubbing his knees like he was getting or paying the damn ticket. He had one hand on the door handle as the cop came walking up like he was going to jump out and run. The officer kindly asked me for my license but rudely asked Caleb for some identification also. After Caleb lied to the officer and told him that he misplaced it while moving, the officer started looking in the back of my car. At this time, Caleb began to sweat harder and had turned toward the door like he was going to make a run for it any second. I began to worry also as the cop refused to give up his search. I had heard so many stories about the police and their hatred for young black men. Some say that they would go as far as planting drugs on them just to lock them up.

Caleb and I got more nervous when several police surrounded us. They made us get out the car and lay on the ground while the officers and their dogs attacked my car. I was irate, thinking, How does a person get pulled over for speeding then made to lie on the ground like a dog? After what seemed like forever on a cold ground, we were told that we would be going down town to the station.

After sitting for hours in a holding cell, I was finally told that I was under arrest for possession of a controlled substance. They said how much and what it was, but I had never heard such terms. After managing to get a clear answer to my slew of questions, I realized that they were talking about some drugs. I smoked blunts, but I didn't know anything about the drugs that they told me I possessed. These men went on and on for hours asking me "Where did you get the dope?" I began to curse louder. "I don't know anything about no motherfucking drugs, so how can I tell you anything."

My stress level was through the roof, and I was so frustrated that I was unaware of what was really going on. I then demanded to see my boyfriend. The men then left and shortly returned with a lost Caleb. "Baby, tell these fools that I didn't have any drugs," I said, waiting confidently on his response. For some weird reason, Caleb just stood there with his green eyes piercing through my soul and said nothing; not one damn word. I then went into a rage, "Nigga, tell them that the drugs weren't mine."

I didn't know if Caleb ever answered me. I only remembered waking up in a position that didn't allow my body to move. My guess was that I blanked out, which meant that somebody had pissed me off. Before gathering the rest of my thoughts, I was bothered by a masculine-sounding woman telling me that I had a visitor. She kindly unbuckled my feet and escorted me to a room of windows. With half opened eyes, I lifted my head to see Big Belle and Cat shaking their heads back and forth. "Baby, what happened?" said a concerned Big Belle. The bitch beside her had no clue. "You know what happened, Mom. That girl has been dealing with drugs and drug people. She even brought such evilness into your home." I couldn't believe that Baby Cat could be so cold and selfish through any situation. She doesn't stop there; she continues with more bull, "I went into prayer after hearing about this thug that she brought around your house. God then gave me a revelation that something was going to happen that would cause great hardship in the family. Here it is, money to get this troubled child out of trouble." Catalina continued to down me in order to make herself look like she was in the sky.

I just sat wishing that I would be released so that I could whip Cat's ass for the first time. Just the other day, I was all good with Jesus, but now she done caused me to realize that God didn't love me enough to save me. Besides, she was so full of hell that I didn't want no part of her God nor her heaven. "Maybe there are two gods. Come on, Big Belle, pray that our God helps me."

As I sat day after day listening to free lawyers, I became more convinced that this shit was real. I was going to jail for having this nigga's dope in my car. What's really messed up about it is, he has been selling drugs all his life but can't pay ten thousand dollars to get me out. He could never have loved me and be willing to watch me rot in jail for his crime.

I questioned love and as usual my faith. "Why didn't Big Belle say that everything was going to be all right? Does she love me? Has she lost her faith?" My mind was full of insane thoughts, but I was only trying to make some logic of things. Why did God answer Cat's prayer? She obviously prayed for Caleb to be removed from Big Belle's. The preacher always said to be careful what you pray for. While she was praying for him to go away, I was put away. Was Cat so damn righteous that her prayer was to punish the unrighteous?

Thirty days passed and I had hit rock bottom. After praying for several days, I decided to give up on God. Where was he during this time of sorrow? "All I see is darkness." The sun had not shined in weeks. I had become so angry that I couldn't even force out a tear. Anyway, no one had heard my cries so far. Then I started thinking about how Big Belle didn't just sing, "He heard my cry," she sang "I love the Lord; he heard my cry." With this in mind, I began to moan like Big Belle, and I chanted, "Father, help me. I love you Lord, and I surrender my all to you. I will do your will. Father, please get me out of here."

My faith was restored, and I was determined to walk in that courtroom tomorrow with confidence that God would deliver. When I called Big Belle, I had a different attitude. I was confirming that she was coming to my trial and making sure that my baby was OK. Big Belle said that she was riding with Cat but was hesitant when answering me about Marcus Jr. She finally said that he was all right, but I knew that she was holding back something. Since every time that something good happens for me, something bad does also, I knew that a bomb would drop tomorrow after I am cleared of my charges.

Twenty-four months of probation was like music to my ears. I couldn't imagine going to prison for something that I didn't do. Although I hated being locked in that hellhole, I felt like I was in hell again after listening to Catalina brag in her proper-talking language how she paid a topnotch lawyer to help me. The lawyer worked for her church and volunteered his services. She went on and on about how he would be blessed. I just sat in the car, confused, thinking of how I had just finished praising God in my inside voice for helping me; now I was ready to curse Cat out in my outside voice for helping me.

As we got closer to home, Big Belle started crying and nervously begun telling me that Marcus Jr. is not at the house with Darian. "Nita, I'm so sorry, the baby's daddy came with court papers and took the baby with him." I thought that I was going to explode. "Where the hell is Caleb?" I needed to smoke some drugs and borrow a gun ASAP.

I sat in the car and said nothing, for there were too many demons taking over my body. I could feel all hell breaking lose in me. When the car stopped, I ran in the house, hoping that I was having a nightmare and was about to fill my baby with a face full of kisses.

Finally, reality sat in as I paced throughout the entire house. I then sat on my bed and cried like I was at Big Belle's funeral. My baby was gone, and he didn't even know his daddy. Plus there was no telling what bitch he had around him.

I was missing my baby so much that I couldn't think about missing my so-called man that let me take the rap for him. I was angered to think that I lost my baby because I chose to be with a good-for-nothing nigga. I was the one helping him to get out of the gangster life. Why didn't I listen to Big Belle when she said a woman can do bad all by herself. Maybe because she contradicted herself when she also said that "A piece of man is better than no man at all." She must have meant that a piece of d— was better than none at all.

I started back crying hard when Big Belle came to my room. "Nita, can I come in?" I must be grown 'cause Big belle has never asked to come in. "This my house," she always fussed. I didn't answer. I decided to sit and cry until she finished her Jesus speech and leave.

My mind was not on Jesus; it was on the devil. I wanted to break a commandment and kill a couple of men right then. Big Belle must have sensed my corrupted state of mind because she entered with Jesus on her tongue. "In the name of Jesus, help this child." As Big Belle continued to ramble on in prayer, I sat stiff and refused to let any good into my heart.

After prayer, Big Belle noticed my disregard and began to firmly preach to me. "Nita, you sitting over there like you don't know that Jesus is real. Who you think delivered you from that jail cell? They told us you were facing ten years in prison. When you were released, I couldn't help but shout, and you should be shouting too. I know you miss your baby, so do I, but I'm here to tell you that the God I serve is an on time God. He will deliver. Do you hear me? He will, so believe, and you shall receive your blessing."

"Thank you, Jesus." I cried out over and over again. My tears had turned into a river of joy. I was so thankful that, where I was weak, Big Belle was strong. She had taught me so much, but my stubbornness caused me to lock the knowledge away.

When Big Belle left my room, I decided to do as she used to do when I was little. I went into my closet, shut the door, dropped to my knees, and cried "Father, I'm here. Please help me!"

CHAPTER 13

Darian

There I was so consumed in self-pity that I had shut out the fact that others in my family had suffered just as much as I. Poor Darian, he was still handsome, but he seemed to have aged rather quickly. I guess the fact that he wasn't getting any had taken a toll on his youth. It may also have been due to his latest late-night drinks at the club.

The Teaser was the newest adult entertainment club across the water. I couldn't help but notice that my aunt's husband had become a regular. I had been working at the Teaser for a couple of months but had managed to ignore Darian. He didn't seem to know me since I was in costume. I usually wore a long purple wig that hung to my knees. I mainly danced with my back toward the audience, and when I faced them, I swung the hair to cover my face.

I couldn't bear the fact of Darian knowing that it was me. I was ashamed of being a stripper; plus it would be one more thing for Catalina to throw in my face. Then I remembered that he couldn't tell on me because he would be putting himself in the picture, which would get him thrown out. Although I was guilty from getting money this way, I was happy that I was able to pay my own lawyer to get my baby back. Even if I was sinning, God knew my heart.

Friday nights at the Teaser were always pretty good; however, this particular Friday was off the chain. I had decided to wear my white-braided wig that had two huge plaits. I didn't feel like having sore feet, so I danced barefoot all night. Without heels, I was able to out-twirk all the other dancers. My money kept piling up and so did my ego.

By the second half of the night, I had taken off my wig and wore my short, sleek honey-blonde hair. I guess the real hair lovers were in the house because I turned around and noticed that my stage was fuller than ever. Every seat was taken, and the moans of lusting men were filling the room. They sounded like a bunch of demons, but I didn't care as long as they had dollars in their hands.

"Shake it, shake shake it." The beat of D.J. Twine's mix had taken over my head and my butt. I was shaking like I had no worries, when suddenly I bent over to smack a beautiful head of waves with my huger-but-real breasts and swallowed hard as I noticed that the tipper was Darian. When our eyes met, he immediately exited the club but left a huge tip on my stage.

The rest of the night was a blur for me. I hadn't been smoking too much, but after this night, I needed some mind regulation. I sat in the dressing room for at least one hour and got so high. I then sent for some duck and noodles with extra red pepper from the Chinese joint. This Chinese food always done something magical to me when I was high. It was ran by black people so was referred to as Chinese soul food. Their crab Rangoon looked like cracklings but were so good.

I was getting ready to pull off when Darian's car pulled on the side of me. "Nita, can I talk to you?" Darian had a sad look on his face, so I couldn't turn him down. Besides, my cover was blown anyway. "What's the story on Kaishira?" asked an obviously desperate, no-coochie-getting Darian. I almost choked partially because Kaishira was the biggest whore at the Teaser and because he must think that I am a non-caring whore. Catalina and I may not have agreed on most issues, but she is my aunt, and blood is thicker than water. If I hear that Kaishira a.k.a. Kaish has screwed my uncle, I will knock her block off. Darian then stopped my angry thoughts by giving me some sad story about how she was nice to him when he felt the lowest ever in his life.

I realized that Darian had something more bothering him besides the fact that his wife ain't being a wife. I thought that his job was all good, but after he begins to tell me about his latest news, I couldn't help but become nervous for him. Darian said that a project that he designed had gone bad. He said that his company had placed him on an indefinite leave pending investigation results.

I couldn't believe that Darian was spilling his guts to me. He went on to tell me that his father had to convince another physician to change results that indicated abuse of pain meds in Darian's blood. Evidently he was injured along with other coworkers while testing his project.

I thought that he was finish venting when he wiped tears from his eyes and said that Catalina had fallen in love with some foreigner from South Africa. He said that she wanted to find herself. I became very confused. How could Cat leave her beautiful husband for some funny-talking, black-ass African.

I found myself cursing about Cat to Darian. I understood why he felt the need to do what he was doing. Darian stopped me from downing Cat and said that he deserved this because everything was his fault. He said that he and Cat could not get over the death of their son because she never wanted to talk about it. He said that she would storm out any time he brought up the tragedy. I tried convincing him that it wasn't his fault, but he cried so hard that I could hardly make out his words. When I figured out what he was saying, I felt his pain. He said that he and Cat had been arguing over a house on the night that they lost the baby. Catalina wanted a home that was not affordable with their income. Darian said that he was against borrowing money from his parents. Catalina didn't want to take no for an answer, so she decided to punish him by angrily storming downstairs. However, she didn't make it before falling and losing their son.

Oh my god. Darian felt like he was the reason why the baby was lost. He also believes that it's his fault that Catalina left him for another man. Why had God chosen me, a girl with a messed-up mind, to be in this situation right now. On one hand, I wanted to give Darian good advice that may help him get his wife back, and on the other, I wanted to pull his beautiful self close to me and show him how he should be appreciated. "So now do you see why I asked about your coworker?" At that point, Darian could have asked me anything. I felt so bad for him and was at his mercy. "Darian, I know things look bad, but you have to hold on. Everything will be OK. Getting involved with a slut like Kaishira will not wipe away your pain; it will make things worse."

When I asked Darian if he had been going to church, I felt like a hypocrite since I hadn't been in forever either. Darian answered me with pure weakness. He said that he was ashamed to go around the people of the Vessel since he had been so low. This was exactly what pissed me off about church people. They should be holy enough to recognize that someone feels low, and instead of pushing their gospel foot in the persons head, they should become humble and help them get back up.

Trying to help a heart-broken Darian, I suggested that he go to church Sunday with Big Belle and me. I knew that he could use some ole-time religion just like me. I needed the prayers of the faithful. I didn't want to be a stripper forever.

Big Belle had a heavy heart these days, but Darian and I going to church with her Sunday made her very happy. She was shouting during devotion. The moment her soulful voice yodeled out the first line of her hymn, I started crying and so did Darian. Next thing I knew, I was on my feet with my eyes tightly shut, yelling, "I know I am a child of God." Everybody repeated after me just like they did Big Belle; unfortunately, that was the only line that I knew. I never knew what the ole folks would say but I hummed along anyway. So we hummed, and at that moment, everything was OK.

CHAPTER 14

My Testimony

Nearly a whole year had passed, and I was less than one week away from my final custody hearing. The money from the club was great, but I was relieved when Caleb gave me the rest of the money so that I could quit. After paying off the lawyer, I put the rest toward starting my own business. Caleb and I were getting along pretty well. He was so sorry for letting me do jail time and really showed his appreciation. Caleb had been in trouble before, so he would have done at least ten years. I was happy that I saved him; but if I would have had a choice before I done those nerve-wracking thirty days, I would have said, "See you in ten."

My future was finally looking up. I was more than halfway finish with beauty school. I had decided that, when I received my license, that I would turn my braid and dread shop into a real beauty shop. The name of my braid shop was Zo's Rows but would change to Zo's Rows and Style." I was already full of ideas when Big Belle sent me to the basement to get a box of momma's things. I guess, since I was becoming a real hairdresser, she figured that I should have it. The box was full of old Marcel waving irons and pin curl clips. I chuckled, thinking my momma was doing her thang back in the day. I then thought about using her stuff as decorations for my "times have changed" wall in a corner of my salon. This corner would consist of the old equipment and portraits of old stiff hairdos.

I was about to put the box away when a picture fell out of a slit of the box. On the picture was an attractive man standing with his arms wrapped around my momma. They were at some club called Club Ice. Momma had on some skin-tight Daisy Dukes with four-inch wedge heels. The guy, who looked like Aunt Margaret's description of Z, was fine as heck. He had on a bright green shirt with matching slacks and shoes. His dreads were in a ponytail that accented his high cheekbones. They were so cute together. I decided to keep this picture of Z and my momma. He may not be my daddy but was the closest thing to a daddy that I had known. Besides, his name was Z, and I'm Zonita; plus he kind of looked like me.

Caleb and I had planned a full weekend of adult fun. We were confident that my baby would be coming home for good that Monday after court. We decided to get partying out of our systems so that we could devote ourselves into being great parents to my little boy. Instead of fussing about how bad he was and how I wish I had a babysitter so that I could kick it, I should have been thanking God that he was alive, healthy, and just simply with me.

After closing the shop Friday night, Caleb and I decided that we would get a room on the nice side of town, eat fancy food, and make love all night long. I was excited but guilty; here I was thanking God that he was about to give my baby back, but I was determined to commit a passionate sin. I wished that I could have been married and therefore not sin, but things just didn't work that way for me.

Caleb had been doing better; however, he still smoked too much, and he had his side hustle. Although he made good money doing dreads in the shop, he had expensive taste. The boy could dress his butt off. He even had me wearing name brand jeans. He brought me a pair of 320-dollar-a-pair jeans to wear this weekend. When I saw the price tag, I almost flipped; but after seeing how they looked on me, I shut up and switched harder.

This night was perfect. Caleb was a perfect gentleman. He opened doors and filled my head with compliments. We ate at an expensive Japanese restaurant of his choice. He said that he knew I loved seafood and heard that this place was exceptional. After dinking several glasses of lime hot sake, I was in the mood. I began to look in Caleb's green eyes as if it was the first time. He just smiled back and said how beautiful I was and how lucky he was to have me in his life. I had to pat tears off my lashes, as he started crying. He told me how I changed his life.

Before Caleb could get even more sensitive, the chef was standing before us with a griddle that took up half our table. He surprisingly lit a fire underneath the griddle and placed our food beautifully on top. My lobster was decorated so pretty. I didn't know whether to eat it or just look at it.

Caleb and I were so full that we decided to skip the club scene and go straight to the hotel. The room was beautiful. The bed was shaped like a huge diamond. This room had a personal hot tub, which had wine and glasses sitting on its crystal deck.

Although I was stuffed, I couldn't help but dip one of the fresh strawberries into the chocolate fountain that also sat by the hot tub. Everything was so delicious that I couldn't wait to enjoy it all with my man "Caleb, baby, you have to try these strawberries." I repeated myself a couple of times, but for some reason, Caleb didn't answer. I figured the food must not have agreed with him so he would be awhile.

Finally, Caleb came pimping out the bathroom in nothing but a pair of sexy underwear. They were white with little tiny words on the crotch. As Caleb got closer, I tried reading his underwear, but he distracted me when he ripped my clothes off and pulled me into the hot tub. We ate chocolate-dipped strawberries and drank until we were in another world. Every time I tried to remove Caleb's sexy underwear, he didn't let me; instead, he pleasured me over and over in every other way possible.

Caleb got out the tub before me and turned off the rest of the lights. I then noticed that the writing on his underwear glowed in the dark. He stood his little sexy ass in front of me as if he was waiting on me to say something. I laughed as my tipsy ass almost fell into him as I got closer to his underwear. I couldn't believe that Caleb's underwear said Will You Marry Me? This thuggish boy had done something so romantic. On top of that, he had the nerve to be standing there like he was nervously waiting for my answer. "Yes, boy." I didn't know what I was doing or saying, but it felt wonderful.

Monday was finally here, and after talking to my lawyer, I was ready for God to fight my battle. I was even more assured when I walked into the court room and saw all my supporters. Big Belle hadn't been feeling her best but was there sitting by Darian. Catalina didn't come. It wasn't like I had expected her. Darian was more like family than Cat was. I didn't need her. There was my boo, Caleb, and a dozen of our church members. One of the members patted me on my back and said that Rev. Lipe sent up a powerful prayer in the parking lot before they entered. She then confidently said, "God got this." I believed her with all my heart.

"Marcus, can I talk to you?" I knew that Marcus wasn't happy about me getting Junior Back, but I had hoped that he would understand. I didn't owe him any explanation, but I tried explaining myself anyway. "I know that you think that I'm a bad mother, but I didn't have any drugs. I took care of Marcus Jr. by myself. Yes, you sent money, but I was the one up at night when he was sick, not you." I then went on to tell him that I wanted him to be a part of our child's life. Marcus just stood there like I wasn't talking to him. I wasn't about to let him take my joy; I had my baby, and that was all that mattered.

Back at the house, Big Belle had cooked a celebration dinner. She fixed Marcus Jr.'s favorite mac and cheese. She also fried chicken and made greens and fried corn, which are a couple of my favorites. Marcus Jr. ate like he was starving. I guess his daddy's white girlfriends didn't know how to cook like Big Belle. After eating, he displayed some of his newly acquired smart aleck mouth. I told him that it was time for bed, and he replied as if he was grown, "Man, I ain't even sleepy." I knew I needed to whip him, but I just laughed at my baby getting older.

After making Marcus go to bed, Caleb and I decided to tell Big Belle that we were engaged. I didn't have a ring yet, but it was official. My heart wanted this man. An older Big Belle was easier to please. I knew that she didn't believe that Caleb was the one for me, but she was happy that I was taking a huge step in life. She didn't have many questions, and we didn't have many answers. We didn't have a clue when we would get married but figured it would be in the next couple of years.

The next six months flew by, and I had so many plans for my optimistic life. The biggest thing was preparing for opening day of Zo's Rows and Style. After passing my licensure, I had a head full of steam. I spent hours making the shop bigger and better. God was really blessing me. I had a full booking as soon as I advertised the reopening of the salon.

Zo's Rows and Style was packed on opening day. Everybody wanted to see and experience my new ideas. It was my time to start a new trend. Big Belle even showed up to get her little fragile hair whipped. After making Big Belle look like she had hair, I told her that instead of being fried, dyed, and laid to the side that she alive, toned, and her bounce is on.. She then laughed and said that I sounded like a rapper. I giggled back thinking, I get it from my momma.

When I made it home late that Saturday night, I was glad that Marcus Jr. was ready to pass out 'cause so was I. Caleb went to hang out with his friends. I must have been tired because normally I hated when he hung out. He always came home high as a kite and therefore misses church. Nothing was keeping me from church; I couldn't wait to get up and testify about everything that the Lord had done for me.

First giving honor to God, pastor, members, visitors, and friends. This was my first time testifying, but I had listened to Mrs. Polkey's introduction every Sunday. I then started to cry but managed to choke out my words, "God has been good to me. I could never praise him enough. Just a couple of years ago, I was wrongly jailed. I felt like giving up, and many times, I sided with the devil. I said and thought such cruel things. However, my God has pity on me, a filthy, dirty person like me. I am so thankful that all of you, along with my momma, Big Belle, prayed for me.

"God didn't stop there. While I was gone, my baby boy was taken from me. I fought for a year to get him back. During this year, my heart was so heavy as I became a dancer at a club to raise money along with all types of other sinful things. Again, I'm thankful that I was delivered from the club and God let me receive money elsewhere. He doubled what I had which allowed me to open a beauty shop, which has grown in a short period of time. God made a way for me when I couldn't see a way. I just can't stop thanking him for all he's done.

"He even blessed me to find true love. My boo, Caleb, and I will be getting married soon. I am so excited to see what God gone do next. I ask each of you to continue praying that my faith grows stronger in the Lord."

By the time I finished with my testimony, the praise music was thumping and the saints of God were jumping. Shouts of glory filled the church. Big Belle just rocked; she didn't jump anymore, but her soulful cries of "Hallelujah" was enough to keep the spirit moving.

CHAPTER 15

Cat is Back

I never thought that Caleb and I would still be engaged after three years had passed. I hoped we would have been married, but every time it came up, we both pulled back. I think that he knew that he was not cut out to be a husband. I wanted to be married but did not want to end up divorced like Catalina and Darian. If I was to have a husband, I wouldn't do him like Catalina did poor Darian, and if Caleb did that to me, I would make sure he wasn't able to be with anyone else. This was probably one of the reasons for us to pull back too. Once we're married, it's going to be to 'til death do we part.

As I continued to think about my marriage woes, I started thinking about some of Big Belle's stories of how women in the South kept their men. Big Belle once told me that Aunt Claire buried her after sex cleansing towel in the backyard. She said that's what women did to keep their men from ever being with another woman. I would laugh at this nonsense but was curious if it worked. She had me rolling when she said that grandpa Rufus was scared to eat her spaghetti. With her head high and her butt poked, she said, "Child, I didn't have to put no hex on him to keep him if you know what I mean."

None of the women liked Big Belle back in her day because she had a big butt that turned all the men's heads. Some of the women even called her fat. Big Belle said she would just laugh and chant seductively, "Don't nothing, but a dog want a bone." That's how she got the name Big Belle.

Well I didn't need voodoo to keep a man either. However, maybe Darian should have buried a pair of Catalina's panties or just kept a pair at his house and pray she come back to him. Poor Darian will probably never get over Cat; he was too consumed with guilt.

Big Belle was excited that Catalina was finally coming home to visit. She did seem saddened after hearing that Cat and Darian were officially divorced but said she had faith that God wasn't done with them yet. As for me, I hoped they would work thing out also, but I wasn't excited that the boogie bitch was coming home.

Catalina was really high and mighty now. On the latest cover of the Vessel's magazine, is "The Rise of Evangelist Catalina." She was beautiful and looked like she had started back to wearing lashes and makeup. For the past few years, her hair was always in a bun; now it was draping with flowing loop curls.

Since Catalina had changed, I wondered if her sermons had. The article "The Rise of Evangelist Catalina" was very interesting. It talked about how her years of dedication to the church and the mission had allowed God to use her in a big way. She traveled all over the world to help start churches. These churches all derived from the Vessel. Catalina was the main speaker for the first month and filled the churches. Everyone wanted to be blessed by the queen of the Vessel.

Catalina's sermon in this issue was called "Wrapped." Catalina had a way with words. She used a beautifully wrapped gift as her example. She somehow proved that once we open the gift, the previous excitement is short lived. We then use the gift until it's no longer usable or we sat it somewhere and never use it. She then compares the gift to the beautiful gift that God gave us. The gift is Jesus. Just like the Christmas gift, the gift is gorgeous while it is properly wrapped. She then goes on to state that when we unwrap our gift (Jesus), we are, doomed until we get wrapped back up. Our gift is having the choice of being wrapped up, tied up, and tangled up in Jesus. All we have to do is ask, and he will wrap us up over and over again. She ended by saying that our best weapon against evil is to stay wrapped. That was the first time I ever read her entire article, and surprisingly, she was very enjoyable.

The house smelled great. Big Belle managed to cook a feast. She really wanted to please Catalina. She even had me washing all her fancy dishes that hadn't been used in years. "Make that boy sit down somewhere." Big Belle was too serious. She didn't want Marcus messing up her perfectly cleaned house. I grabbed Marcus by the hand and decided to take him to the park. I knew that he was too hyper to not touch anything.

I had considered staying away, period, but I was anxious to let Catalina know that Caleb and I were getting married, so I wouldn't be living in sin much longer. Maybe she wouldn't be ashamed of us and would spend more time with her momma. Big Belle's other seven kids rarely visited or called. Aunt Margaret called the most because she was the nosiest. Angrily, I thought, if something happened to Big Belle, they would all be at her funeral screaming and shit.

After cleaning Marcus Jr. up and convincing Caleb to dress less thuggishly, I went to help Big Belle with final preparations. As I set the table, I imagined Cat coming through those doors, moving her slender hips from side to side and, while batting her lashes, say some something cute and smart aleck. That Cat whom was down here on earth with us is long gone. Now Catalina's feet will never touch this floor; she's going to fly in here like an angel on a cloud.

When Catalina arrived, she was actually switching like the old Cat. She had on a dress, but it was a clinging maxi dress. She actually looked thirty instead of fifty. She even hugged my boy who had no clue who she was. She never had anything to do with him, which was understandable.

"Mother, I have someone that I want you to meet," said an anxious Catalina. She then went to the door and ushered in this older white man. I figured he was one of her mission workers. When she introduced Dale as her man, I thought Big Belle was going to fall out of her chair. I couldn't tell if she was getting ready to curse or pray. There was nothing but curse words on my tongue. I couldn't believe who she had traded Darian in for.

After listening to Catalina and Dale talk about their love for one another and how it was a part of God's plan, I felt nauseous. I began thinking that the people who read her articles or listen to her while she preaches may hear her words. However, I knew the real Cat. So when it comes to hearing this Catalina person, I became deaf.

If Catalina was "Wrapped," she would be with her husband instead of this first-time-going-black white man. She even let this man tell her what to do. The Cat that I knew was always independent. She wore her hair however she wanted to. When I mentioned the highlights in her hair, she said that Dale didn't like her dark brown hair. "Well, your ends need to be clipped off. If you are going to get damaging highlights," I said, being the one who always noticed hair problems. She properly replied that Dale wants her hair long, and she will not be getting a haircut.

The more I listened to Catalina, the madder I got. I then changed the subject and brought up Caleb and my engagement. When Catalina completely ignored my announcement, I decided to give her a much needed piece of my mind. After convincing her to come out on the porch with me, I poured out all my frustrations. I basically told her that she was no better than anybody and how wrong she was for leaving Darian. I also let her know that I didn't think she would get to heaven any quicker than anyone else with her fake ass. She didn't even get the Holy Ghost like Big Belle and the Baptist preachers. I was so mad that I continued to say so many cruel statements.

My lecture must have worked because Catalina broke down. She started working her neck like the ole Cat. She tried snapping, telling me that I didn't know anything about her life with the church. She fed me some line that Darian was holding her back from doing what God had for her to do. I lashed out again, causing her to break down in tears. I actually began to feel sorry for Cat when she told me that she had to get away from Darian so that she could forgive him. "Because of you, I can never have kids" is what Catalina said every day in her mind. Darian had no clue that Catalina was injured during the loss of the baby and would never be able to conceive again. She said that leaving him helped her come to peace with it. She dedicated her body and soul to the church only. That is until she met Dale. "Well, why you stay away from us?" I cried. She then told me that she couldn't be around us because she was angry.

Catalina had done what Big Belle always preached, but God took her baby. "There you were, Nita, a bad girl, and God let your baby live. I now know from prayer and studying that his plan is always good. I had to go through those trials so that I could help others come to Christ." I couldn't believe it, but I heard Catalina's every word. She spoke like Cat instead of evangelist Catalina.

CHAPTER 16

Family Reunion

When I was younger, I didn't give a heck about family. However, since I was approaching thirty, I started looking at life differently. I had always thought that as long as I had Big Belle, that I needed no one else. Now as I look at my little man, who was getting so big, I realized that I wanted more for him. I didn't want him to be angry growing up as I was. I wanted him to love his life and who he came from.

I didn't know anything about my cousins that lived all over the country. We even had family in Trinidad. Big Belle often told me that I looked like the family from over there. I guessed that they were dark skinned.

It had been years since the Walkers had a reunion, which we normally orchestrated. We had never been to a Daniels reunion, which was Big Belle's maiden family. After receiving the paper in the mail, which we had also received many years prior, I decided to talk Big Belle into going. I pictured Big Belle, Caleb, Marcus Jr., and I having a ball down in Mississippi. If Catalina and Darian were still together, they could come too. I doubted that the white man would want to go down there. Plus Aunt Claire's family is not known for liking white folk.

After getting everything packed into the car, we were on our way. I was excited to drive my new car down the highway. The shop had been successful. I was able to buy a car and save money for a new house. I figured that I would leave Big Belle's one day.

Marcus Jr., who had reached his preteen years, was such a huge help to Big Belle. Big Belle walked on a cane now; but Marcus, who had gotten taller than her, helped her with every move, especially with our many bathroom stops. Big Belle had a weak bladder, and Caleb drank beer, so it was either him or her that needed to stop.

By the time we arrived at our hotel, I was drained. I asked Big Belle if we could rest before going to Aunt Claire's. An anxious Big Belle just nodded her head like she knew I would say that. From what I had heard about the people down here, I knew that they would have plenty partying left whenever we got there. I also knew that Big Belle didn't plan to stay in the hotel with us, which was fine with me. Her and Marcus Jr. could sleep with the mosquitos.

"Girl, look at you. Them hips so wide, I can't see who's behind ya." Why in the heck would the first person I see have to be Aunt Margaret. My hips had gotten smaller since I had been working out. Nevertheless, there went my confidence. I thought I was going to be the finest thing Mississippi ever seen, and there she goes bursting my bubble.

My deflated bubble was short lived, as I ran into Aunt Nicety, whose real name was Nedra. She was one year younger than momma. Big Belle said that Aunt Nicety was so particular when she was young that if someone touched her food, she would throw it away. This caused everyone to call her nice nasty. "Nita, you still look like you nineteen. How old are you?" I smiled big and said, "I'm thirty, Aunt Nicety."

Big Belle sat in the house with Aunt Claire. Aunt Claire was just a couple of years older than Big Belle but wasn't able to get around at all. She had some of everything wrong with her. Diabetes was her worse enemy. It had affected her whole body. I felt sorry for her but stayed far away. It was depressing to hear her cry about never seeing us.

Caleb and Marcus Jr. seemed to fit in well. Marcus Jr. played basketball all evening, and Caleb drank beer and smoked blunts around back with my country cousins. I didn't like the country men cousins at all. They knew that Caleb was my man; but every time they got a chance, they would say, "Girl, you sho you our cousin? You fine as wine." That's why I decided to stay away from the drunks in the back.

The women were getting their drinks on too. Aunt Margaret and her daughter, Misty, were two sheets in the wind. Aunt Nicety must have spoken up for me because Aunt Margaret gave me a compliment. "Nita, girl, you know I just be kidding with you. You are so pretty just like my sister was." I knew she was drunk, but she seemed sincere. She then went and on about how she loved me and all her family. Now here comes her bipolarity. "We all knew that Big Belle had her picks; that is why me and mine stayed away. We love momma, but she not right for loving Bonita and Cat more than the rest of us."

Suddenly I was no longer feeling the love. Big Belle always said that a drunk tells his or her true feelings. I hated the fact that family can't just party. It's always a fight at some point or another. Somebody was always jealous 'cause so-and-so got a better job, car, and a better body. Blood is supposed to be thicker than water, but I can't tell that it is. Family would rather see a stranger do better than their own kin.

I just might have to go in the house or to my car before I have to slap this b—, I thought to myself as Aunt Margaret tells Aunt Nicety to shut up while Aunt Nicety is trying to talk to me about her hair. Instead I was the bigger person, ignored Aunt Margaret and started up a good conversation. I could always say something good about hair and my new inventions. I believed that if you had one hair strand left, I could save it. However, after several experiments that failed, I decided to launch a new trend called "don't save it, shave it." Aunt Nicety wanted to hear all about it while Aunt Margaret made sarcastic remarks after every sentence.

I was used to dealing with unbelievers like Aunt Margaret, but for the most part, everyone had been optimistic. My "don't save it shave it" trend consisted of six to twelve months. The balding, hormonal and older women were placed on the twelve-month program, and the others with regular hair growth were placed on the six-month program. I formulated new shampooing techniques along with regular scalp manipulations that changed throughout the program. Each client was sent home with hair workout instructions that instructed them on how to do home massages and a list of their future appointments.

Aunt Nicety was sold. She said that she would have no problem coming home to Big Belle's for a year if she didn't have to wear wigs the rest of her life. I was excited to help Aunt Nicety but also scared that she may have been too bald too long. To save it, there must be some hair to shave.

After discussing the price of my services with Aunt Nicety, Aunt Margaret gets extremely agitated and says such disrespectful things to me. "Girl, you are just like yo momma. You will do anything for the ole mighty dollar." Next thing I knew, Big Belle was hollering and crying, "Nita, what's wrong with you? Why are you cursing at your own flesh and blood like this?"

I guess I must have had one of my blanked-out moments. I knew that Aunt Margaret caused me to become full of rage, but everything else was a total blank. As I looked around, I noticed family standing, staring, and shaking their heads at me. I guess I must have really went off. I felt horrible, but from what I remember, it was her fault. It tripped me out. How can she get away with talking to me any kind of way? It's obvious that I snapped on her as retaliation. Now Big Belle was over there, crying like I done killed the woman.

It didn't take long for me to realize that pleading my case to a bunch of one-zone-minded people was getting me nowhere. So I decided to get my boys and leave. Caleb was so high that he was ready to lay it down. Marcus Jr., on the other hand, wanted to stay with his country cousins. They could stay out all night since there were no police, and everybody knew everybody, so the kids were safe. If I wasn't so mad, I would have left him there.

I was so relieved to be on our way to the hotel. I didn't want to spend another second with those simple-minded people. "Tomorrow, Big Belle is on her own. We'll find something in town to do." I figured it was best that I stay away since my attitude is so bad, to let them tell it.

We weren't ten minutes away when an ambulance passed us, moving out in the opposite direction. At this point, my stomach got all upset, and I could feel that something was wrong with my family. My consciousness was saying that, because of my extreme retaliation, something bad had to happen. Big Belle was so upset. What if she had a heart attack? Several bad thoughts crossed my mind, causing me to turn around and go back.

My heart rate got faster as my bad feeling was confirmed. In the front of Aunt Claire's house were the ambulance and a bunch of hysterical people. As I walked toward the house, I prayed that it was there for anybody but Big Belle. My other loves were with me, so the only other person I really cared about was Big Belle.

The cruelty in Misty's voice as she met me at the door scared me even more. She was blaming me, so it's either her momma or Big Belle. Aunt Claire already had one foot in heaven, so I couldn't have caused her to die.

I didn't have to pray too hard. God knew that I wanted it to be Aunt Margaret on the stretcher, not my Big Belle. "Let me through," I shouted as I saw my love lying there so fragile on the stretcher. She was being pushed to the ambulance, and I couldn't tell if she was dead or alive.

After hours of waiting impatiently, the doctors finally told us that Big Belle had suffered a stroke. I had possibly killed my Belle. They said that her health wasn't the best. Her heart was only functioning at 10 percent, and her kidneys were shutting down fast. They predicted six months if she didn't have surgery but said that she "was too fragile for two major surgeries."

The devil is a liar. Big Belle was awake and ready to get out the hospital bed in less than twenty-four hours. The only thing stopping her was the fact that she couldn't move her legs. The doctors explained that the stroke caused damage to her brain that limited her movement. He explained to me that when she is released from that hospital that she would need to be put in a nursing home for rehabilitation. I thought to myself, "Big Belle ain't going for that." From the looks of things, she may have no choice. I couldn't take care of her and work. As I thought about work, I realized that I would have to leave Big Belle down there. As mad as I was at Aunt Margaret, I was grateful that she said that she would stay.

I prayed and cried the entire way home. Caleb and Marcus Jr. were scared to talk to me; guess they knew I was devastated. It seemed like every time I relaxed on prayer, something else happened. At this moment, I had a brain flash of Big Belle dying. If she dies, who gone pray for me and mine? My faith had gotten stronger but not strong enough to be without Big Belle's prayers. She is so strong. Even though she couldn't move from a hospital bed, she still managed to sing and ole hymn that had the Holy Spirit moving through the hospital. I didn't shout, but I cried and praised with her as she sang, "If I go home to be with Jesus, don't be sad 'cause with my Jesus I'll be glad." Big Belle sang like dying was a piece of cake for her. She was more concerned for the weak in faith like me. Big Belle must have known that heaven would be her home. She felt that she had been a good and faithful servant. She had attended church my entire life.

Now I was realizing that when Big Belle die, if I wanted to see her again, I would have to get right and go to church all the time too. I didn't have a problem with that, but I hated to give up some fun stuff at thirty. The preacher always preaching about "You can't serve Jesus and the devil; you choose. Jesus offers peace, and the devil offers fun." Well, when you're young, fun seems like the better choice.

CHAPTER 17

Zatron

Big Belle made a liar out of everybody. Two years had passed, and her heart was still ticking. She stayed in rehab for six months. After realizing that she would never walk again, she decided to come home. She really didn't like the fact that she wasn't actually going to her old house, but it was evident that she couldn't live alone.

Big Belle could not take complete care of herself, so moving in with me was her best option. It was me or one of her children who lived farther away. I didn't know how long she had left, so I wanted her to be happy. Most of her kids were too bitter, and as for Catalina, well, she is just Catalina. She don't even eat meat, and Big Belle loves fried chicken.

Trying to take care of Big Belle, run after a teenager, and run the shop by myself was too much to handle. Caleb was no help. We still were not married, mainly because he hadn't grown up. He was still running around with Zatron and partying all night. He really acted like a kid when he often threatened to leave after our many fights. I was fed up with Caleb and pissed him off with one of Big Belle's lines: "Gone then, you got diamonds in your back. You look better going than you look coming." Big Belle was so smart to come up with all her sayings. I couldn't believe how I had managed to remember and understand so many of them.

As we sat around the house one Sunday afternoon, I thought my eyes were going to get stuck in my head. I couldn't help but roll them at Caleb and Zatron as they sat watching football on my new flat screen. "They're hustling asses can stay high but never have a dime to their name." No matter how hard I tried, I couldn't help but complain. I was at a point in my life that I didn't care if I had a man or not. "Hell, maybe if he left, I could get a man instead of a thirty-five-year-old boy."

Zatron got the nerve to ask me if I'm going to his daddy's coming home party. He said that his father was supposed to do life but would be getting out after doing twenty years in the federal pen. Before I could answer, Caleb blurted out from the other room, "We gone turn up for your pops." Zatron then looked at me like "I guess you going." Caleb thinks that he runs me. I often wondered how a broke-ass nigga gone tell me anything.

Caleb was so excited about us getting our own house. However, he was not equally excited about the bills. He rarely worked at the shop and paid no bills. What money he made on his couple of hustles kept me from supplying his habits. Caleb's actions caused me to feel so defeated. I knew that God would give me what I needed, but I wanted so much more. The longer I stay with Caleb, the longer it was going to take me to accomplish my goals.

As I continued to listen to Caleb and Zatron brag about how much money the jail bird's party gone cost; the more upset I got. Zatron got lord knows how many baby mommas, and I bet he is not taking care of any of his kids, I thought. Some dumb woman taking care of him just like I'm for Caleb.

Caleb had been throwing the thousands he gave me when I got out of jail in my face for years now. I angrily tell myself, "How many car payments, house payments, utility bills, and on and on have I paid since then?" Now he is sitting over there, talking about his new outfit that he'll be wearing to the party. "Maybe I will go so I can show off my thickness. Hell, I may meet some older dude with a job." I couldn't believe that I was at that point. I loved Caleb, but he and Zatron are doomed. They have settled with a life of being supported by women.

Caleb smoked a blunt on the way to the party. He couldn't function unless he smoked. As for me, I gave up blunts. I was focused on having something more in my life. I had started drinking wine and found myself needing a glass or two every night to deal with the madness of my household. I hadn't been to the club in forever, so I figured I would get in a corner and sip on a bottle of wine. Then I would be able to do my thick girl stroll around the club.

Obviously, Caleb and I were late because the club was packed. Zatron must have been waiting on our arrival because he bomb rushed Caleb as soon as we stepped through the doors. "Come on, man. We back in the VIP." I told Caleb to go ahead without me. I had seen an old friend of mine. He was so eager to get to the blunt fest that he didn't care what I did.

"Hey, Nita girl, you look great!" Cassey didn't look too bad herself. She was skinny but shapely, and her face looked the same as it did in high school. After complementing each other repeatedly, we decided to get a table and have a drink.

I felt relieved to hear all about Cassey's problems. Her husband was as much as a deadbeat as Caleb was. At least she was married to her deadbeat. I couldn't get that far.

By the time Cassey finished her story about her abusive husband, we had drank an entire bottle of wine. As I started to tell her about my issues, she stopped me and said, "Hold that thought. We gone need another bottle."

While Cassey was gone to the bar, I decided to scope out the crowd. There were some handsome men eyeballing me, but they looked no older than twenty-five. Oh god, I shouldn't have looked I thought as this fine thang comes walking toward me. I became nervous of Caleb seeing the dude trying to get with me but figured jealousy might help him. Maybe he would get his act together if he knew that his woman was still hot.

Yes, I was hot. My confidence was through the roof as I listened to the twenty-three-year-old boy tell me how he was young but ready. He told me that he had a good job and was looking for a good woman like me to take care of.

The many glasses of wine that I drank had me blushing too hard. I eventually excused myself and went to the bar where Cassey was. I told him that I had to go to the rest room. I did wonder if he would like all of me as I strolled away from him. As I filled Cassey in, she giggled, telling me that the boy's eyes hadn't left my butt.

We were feeling pretty good from our drinks, so we decided to make our way back to the VIP. I loved the attention, but I didn't want Caleb and Zatron killing some young fine man. Zatron was such a whore. He couldn't wait to ask about my friend. She already had a no-good husband, the last thing she needed was a grown-ass kid. You would think he would know not to ask me about anybody. Surprisingly, Cassey didn't act like he bothered her with his lines, so I went and talked to Caleb.

As I made my way over to the couch that Caleb was on, I noticed he was sitting with a tall good-looking man. "Hey, baby," he said in an excited voice. "This is Zatron's daddy Z." The guy stood up and shook my hand and said, "It's Zatron to you, lovely lady." I didn't know that Zatron was a junior, but I was more intrigued with the fact that Caleb called him Z.

After filling Cassey in with all the details about the Z that was involved in my momma's death, she had convinced me to talk to him and find out if he was the same Z. After drinking three bottles of wine, I was feeling too emotional to question this stranger that could change everything that I know about my life.

I was so deep in thought that I didn't notice Z walking toward me. He wasted no time telling me that he couldn't take his eyes off of me. He then went on to say that I looked just like a woman that he once loved dearly. He was a big, strong handsome man, but at that moment, he looked very weak. Words couldn't describe my feelings.

I'D RATHER GO TO HELL THAN THE HEAVEN THAT YOU'RE IN

I was speechless after confirming that he was the Z that was with my momma.

We didn't get far into the conversation before I realized that he knew just who I was. Zatron Jr. had already filled him in. He knew before he walked over to me that I was Zonita, Bonita's daughter. I was so frustrated that my mind became blank. I wanted to ask this man so many questions, but my brain was frozen. I couldn't pray about it because I was too tipsy to concentrate on talking to God. Anyway, Big Belle always said that Jesus knows all about it, so "Jesus handle this".

Zatron Jr. interrupted our conversation to introduce his daddy to some lady. Cassey decided to go home. She signaled the call-me sign. Guess she had enough of flirting with Zatron and was ready to go home and get beat. As for Caleb, he had started shooting pool. He said one more game and then we could leave. Everything in me wanted to leave his ass, but I didn't I just sat patiently. I was on my way to the restroom when Z pulled me to the floor shouting, "Get down." Obviously, there was a shooting. I was so scared. All I heard was Caleb screaming, "Nita."

Everything happened so quickly. The police and ambulances were there in minutes. It took me a minute to realize that Zatron Jr. had been killed. They were taking him on a stretcher, but his eyes were rolled back, and Caleb was crying like a baby. "Damn, my nigga dead." I looked around the room and couldn't find Z anywhere, and Caleb was too crazy to answer when I asked him.

I didn't know what to do, so I just made Caleb go home with me. They said it wouldn't do any good to go to the hospital because it would be on lockdown. They weren't going to let anyone know what was going on until the investigation was finished.

As Caleb and I finally began walking to our car, I continued to look for Z. Caleb snapped out of his crying and started cursing. He said some mumbo jumbo about how he was going to get them niggas. I was thinking how could he have known who they were; he was shooting pool. I then cursed him and told him that he better tell me what was up or he was not going to my house. He then told me the whole story. Evidently, Zatron never let anyone know when his daddy was getting out of jail nor did he mention Z. Caleb said that

Zatron didn't know why but his daddy was wanted dead by some Italian men. I wondered what Z could have done that could cause someone to want him dead twenty years later. All I knew was that his son is dead, and he is gone.

CHAPTER 18

Caleb

Caleb had not been the same since Zatron died. He may have been a deadbeat, but he had passion, and he was a loving man. Now he acts like he's lost. I told him that we need to go to church, but he wants no part of it. I hadn't been going regularly myself, plus I was becoming a wine head. This is why my son accused me of being a hypocrite when I told him on Saturday night to be prepared for church in the morning. "Momma, Christians don't drink wine." I tried explaining to him that it didn't matter, everybody needed to go so they could get stronger. However, he just became more sarcastic and refused to go.

I was too weak with arthritic hands to whoop a big teenager. He had gotten so tall and looked down on me. There were times that I felt like giving him to his daddy. Lately, I had been overwhelmed with life, so I figured he could be stressing his daddy instead of me.

Caleb didn't know how to be a daddy. He had been with Marcus since he was a few years old but never gained enough respect to be called daddy. In fact, Marcus talks to him like he one of his homies. I believe that Caleb is letting Marcus get high with him. Every time I turn around, Marcus was defending Caleb's dumb actions. I knew that Marcus Jr. would fight Caleb if he put his hands on me, but he still defended him when he was lying to me.

Caleb had been coming in late all the time now. He even smelt like a female had been all over him on several occasions. Marcus Jr. heard one of our many arguments about this and told me that women were just paranoid. He said that one of Caleb's cousins probably hugged him. I had never been the jealous type, so I gave up. However, I was so pissed at my son but did not want to involve him any deeper.

I had been sleeping with this man for ten years and could tell that he was cheating. Caleb had become very insecure since I had made it big at the shop. My salon was the top salon in our area. When I mentioned my accomplishments, he didn't say a word as if he wasn't proud of me. When he did say something, he would rudely change the subject. If I kept talking, he would leave to go hang out with his buddies. Sometimes he even said he was going to check on Zatron's kids. I didn't like the fact that he was going to these bitches' houses, but I couldn't let him think that I too had become insecure.

One day when I got home, Caleb was not there, but his car was in the garage. Big Belle's home aide told me that he left with some man. Big Belle's worker was a young black girl who seemed to be a little rough around the edges, but over all, she was honest and sweet. I knew that Lyndsey was dependable, which is why I stuck with her. We had to let five girls go before getting her.

After Lyndsey described the man that Caleb left with, I couldn't help but to think she was talking about Z. I then sat around for the rest of the evening, angrily waiting on Caleb so that I could put him out. "Shit, if he is dealing with a person that allows others to die for him, I can't have him around my family."

When I woke up that morning, my body shook with fear. Caleb hadn't come home. Although Caleb sometimes stayed out late, he had always come home to sleep with me. My mind began overflowing with negative thoughts. He is probably tired of my bitching, so he stayed with the little young girl that he has been dealing with. I always imagined a young girl because what grown woman that look like something want a nigga like Caleb that's being supported by me. Then I thought, Hell, maybe she wants to support him too. Then I drew the worse conclusion, What if he is dead, and he don't got no ID so the authorities haven't contacted me yet?

Thinking of death made me pray. I started to wake Big Belle, but she was getting weaker by the day. Therefore, I knew that it was my turn to pray. Besides missing church, I had been living pretty well. I had one regular sin, which was fornication, so hopefully God will answer me.

I went to work with my head down and my spirits low. I tried to pull myself together but couldn't make it through the day. Luckily, my assistant, Angie, was a great listener and followed instructions well. She was able to finish my clients while I got on my phone. As I attempted calling the police to file a missing person report, Caleb shows up. He walked into the shop like nothing was wrong. It took all of me not to curse him out. So I didn't even try to question him in fear that I would become unprofessional.

On the way home, I went over my speech to Caleb, who was trailing me in his car. I kept thinking that it may have been best for him to stay where he came from. I was as angry as I had ever been. Well, except for the jail time that he had given me. He could not possibly have a good enough excuse especially since he knows that I was concerned about him being with other women. Why would he do something so stupid? I didn't understand, but I did know that it was over.

"First of all, boo, my phone was dead, and I was too busy concentrating on this money." Caleb was already making me sick with his lies. He must have known that I wouldn't believe a word he said because he instantly pulled out twenty thousand dollars and a speech. "We can get married now. The reason I have been holding back was because I wanted to be able to give you the world. We can go to Jamaica like your aunt did." I knew that the money was illegal, but I was happy that he gave it to me.

After a romantic night of makeup sex, I had forgotten all my questions like "Where did you go, and who did you go with?" I knew that I wouldn't get the truth anyway. Caleb had mastered the art of telling lies and being persuasive. When he explained that he gambled all night long, shooting pool, I actually believed him. At least he was a pro at shooting pool.

I was so caught up in the fantasy of becoming a bride that I had lost touch of reality. Caleb hadn't changed at all; but we were getting older, so I felt it was due time. Our plans were made rather quickly. In two weeks, we planned to get married at the church Sunday following service and leave that Monday for Jamaica.

After getting both Big Belle and Marcus Jr. squared away, we prepared ourselves for our trip of a lifetime. Thankfully, Catalina agreed to keep Big Belle at her house, and Marcus Sr. seemed enthusiastic about spending time with his son.

Jamaica was gorgeous and so were the people. After one day, I had picked up an accent and a new booty-shaking dance. I felt more in love with Jamaica than I did with Caleb. Everybody, including the old folks, were partying, drinking homemade booze, and smoking real herbs. Caleb drank but said that he was through smoking. He said that he felt it was time to concentrate on being a good husband and father.

I didn't miss home at all. I did miss my son and Big Belle, but I could have stayed for at least a month or two. It didn't matter because it was about time to head back to reality. This trip had been a fantasy. I made love to Caleb and felt so free. It was the first time that I had sex, and it wasn't a sin. However, I did wonder if imagining that Caleb was that fine Jamaican boy at the restaurant was a sin? "Who knows? Everything seems to be a sin!" Damn!

Where is Caleb? I thought as I noticed it was almost time to head to the airport. He said that he was going back to get some last-minute gifts, which sounded fishy to me. Being that my mind was in the clouds, Oh well, I thought.

Caleb had been gone so long that we were definitely going to miss our flight, so I called to see when the next flight went out. Thank god there was another one in just a couple of hours. However, it would help if I knew where this boy was.

Before I could get myself all worked up, there was a knock at the door. Every bad thought that I could think of crossed my mind when I opened the door to a policeman. He introduced himself and said that I needed to go with him, and since he had guns, I did just that. Every time I tried asking a question, he just put his hand up as to say shut up. So I just got in the car and shut up!

When we arrived at some weird-looking building, there was Caleb, looking stupid. He explained to the officers that I had nothing to do with his crime. "I know damn well I didn't," I said, feeling very confused. I was both angry and sad as Caleb yelled while they quickly took him away. "It was Z. He set me up." Now I was raging mad. It was Z this whole time.

After waiting hours to visit with Caleb, he decided to fill me in on his new partner in crime. His story was that Z was desperate for his help. He needed Caleb to pick up a package from his cousins in Jamaica so that he could disappear for good. Evidently, Z was fully aware that he would continue to get others around him killed.

I was so pissed at Caleb, but he was my husband, and I loved him. I couldn't deal with him being locked away, so I was determined to get enough money to get him out. I wondered if Z would get him out. Most likely, Z had disappeared, which was for the best. He needed to stay away from me. I was extremely angry at this lowlife. He was responsible for my momma's death, his son's death, and now he had my husband locked up.

It just about killed me to go home without Caleb, but I had to continue to live even if he had been stupid. He told me that he could bond out but had to stay in Jamaica, so I opted to let him stay in jail. I did decide to take the money and hire a lawyer to help with his actual chargers and, therefore, his prison time. I couldn't believe that I was finally married but going home without my husband. I had planned to attend church Sunday morning as a married woman with one less sin to pray for.

The house seemed so empty. Catalina was bringing Big Belle back in a couple of days, and Marcus Jr. wasn't coming home for another week. This was the perfect opportunity to have some friends over to get my mind off of Caleb. A few glasses of wine and women talk would do me some good. I loved my home; it had a nice retro look. Between work and taking care of Big Belle, I hadn't had time for guests.

Cassey had gotten in touch with some of our other buddies, and I invited some of my girls from the shop. They all arrived very quickly. I guess they were excited about coming over or just nosey. I wasn't sure if I wanted to let them know that my husband was really nothing but a thug that was now locked up for God knows how long.

After stuffing ourselves with pizza, we chatted and drank the night away. I listened to so many problems, but none were worse than mine. Their problems consisted of cheating men with abusive, bad attitudes. I wished that my problem was that simple. They talked a lot but picked me for information in between. I couldn't hold my peace any longer, so I let them know that my husband would be gone for a while without letting them know all the details.

Before I embarrassed myself, I decided to end the pity party and cry the night away alone. My faith was too low to pray or ask for prayer. So I decided to hope for something to pray for. My life seemed to be full of unanswered prayers.

CHAPTER 19

Darian Is Deceived

Catalina hung around after dropping off Big Belle. I knew that she was up to something, and it better not had been questioning me. I was full of the devil, so she would most likely get an ass whooping. "So, Nita, Paul is talking about moving into Big Belle's house. Paul was Big Belle's youngest son. I didn't know Uncle Paul well. He moved far away from us and lived his own life. This was the first I had heard of Uncle Paul moving in the house. Normally, I would care, but with my life in shambles, I could have cared less.

Catalina was a sweet, educated, talking devil. She suggested to me that he needed to pay rent or buy the house. "No wonder Big Belle's other kids felt like black sheep." I couldn't stand selfish, money-hungry people. No church could keep Cat from being narcissistic.

After Catalina left, I decided to have a talk with Big Belle. Big Belle didn't look herself. I knew that she believed in God, but she seemed to be giving up on life. All she wanted to do was read her Bible and write. I hated the fact that she only nodded when I spoke. "Belle, do you hear me?" I cried "I don't know what to do." I then went on to tell Big Belle the whole truth about Caleb. I must have had gotten her attention because she began to hum and pray. She then became strong voiced and told me that I needed to pull myself together, and that I had a son to finish raising. She said that it was my choice to marry a man that I knew was no good for me.

Big Belle never said much about Caleb until now. She was really letting me have it. By the time she finished the lecture, I had heard everything from "A hard ass makes a soft head" to "The reason why grease is fatty." Big Belle was starting to get confused, but I understood her, and I was pissed. I knew that she was telling me the truth, but to hell with the truth. How come her God couldn't be there for me? She must have felt my anger and lack of faith because she ended our talk by saying, "Child, you haven't been through no more than the next, so ask yourself who brought them out? Jesus, that's who! So I suggest you get on them chubby knees of yours and pray. Thank him for what he's done for you, and thank him for what he's going to do."

After getting over the shock of Big Belle not only snapping on me but calling me fat, I took her advice and prayed. I tried to feel thankful and sincere. I tried to have a positive outlook on the future and thank God for it.

"Thank you, Jesus," I shouted as Marcus Jr. came walking in the door. He seemed two inches taller and was so handsome just like his daddy. Lately, I hadn't paid much attention to my baby. Unfortunately, I had been too busy trying to turn a thug into husband material. I also buried myself into my shop in an attempt to make it the best shop ever.

I couldn't remember the last time that I hugged my son. For some strange reason, I didn't want to let go. I felt like he was growing apart from me, and I was determined not to let him go. This must have been a premonition because, as soon as our hug ended, he informed me that he was moving with his daddy.

Any other time I would have fought with Marcus, but I was so ashamed about Caleb that I ignored him, hoping that he would change his mind. When he didn't seem to be bluffing, I relied on Big Belle. He didn't listen well to me, but he always heard Big Belle. I told him that I needed him to help out more with her, which only filled my soul with guilt. I was determined to find a way to keep my baby from leaving. I decided to take one day at a time and show my motherly love.

After a long day at work, I pulled into my driveway, and saw Darian driving off. I hadn't seen Darian in forever, so I was curious of why he decided to come by. Marcus Jr. was sitting on the couch when I came in. I knew he thought that he was grown, but he could have said, "Hey, Mom" or something. Instead, I had to start up the conversation.

"Hey, baby, what did Darian want?"

"He wasn't here for you" Marcus rudely replied. At that instant, I felt a blank out coming on, but I prayed Lord don't let me kill this fool. At that time, I understood what Big Belle meant when she said, "I brought you in this world and I will take you out."

Who is this child that is talking to me? Marcus had become a stranger to me. As I went on to explain to him that I wouldn't be putting up with his ungrateful and disrespectful actions, he lashed out at me with years of frustration. "Momma, are you blind? The same ole shit has been going on in front of your face for years now. The fucked-up thing about it is that you have the nerve to question me. Is it possible that you are that dumb?" Here I was getting cursed out by the little nigga that I pushed out my coochie just because I asked one question.

Just when I thought the lashing couldn't get any worse, Marcus begins to tell me all about my nothing-ass man. He told me that I was naïve about everybody. Still very confused about the fact that I only asked why Darian had come by, I tried being humble before someone got hurt and asked the boy to explain himself. He then ended his rage with a horrifying response. He said that Darian was a crackhead.

I was pissed off that Darian's fine ass was on drugs, but I was devastated when I found out that Zatron then Caleb and now Marcus

Jr. had been his suppliers. I was happy that Marcus told me the truth about dealing drugs, but I felt like a failure in that I had to let him go live with his daddy.

Suddenly I was no longer sad that Caleb was in jail. I was full of anger and regrets. How could I have married a man that could do such horrible things under my roof? I had longed for Caleb and cried myself to sleep every single night, but now my tears were dried.

My heart began to ache for Darian. I felt that he would never be able to get over this horrible addiction. I had seen and heard about crackheads my entire life. Unfortunately, I rarely heard of a rehabilitated one. Plus a crackhead seemed to be the lowest of all when it came to drug users. People would say, "So-and-so is on crack, so you better hide your purse." Most of the time, they were also bums, skinny, with a nappy head. So if someone just didn't have it together, they were put in the category of those who were stoned by society.

With a flooded mind of "how can I help" thoughts, I decided to stop by Darian's one evening after work. I knew that he worked during the day, so I figured that I would catch him before he hit the streets.

After arriving at my aunt's old house, I reminisced about how I had always dreamed of living in a house like this with a man like Darian. Before I knew it, I rang the doorbell umpteen times. Feeling discouraged, I decided to leave. Just as I was about to get in the car, a half-awakened Darian hollered, "Hey, Nita, what do you want?"

I was thankful that Darian invited me to come inside but was horrified of his living conditions. The once-beautiful home that Catalina and Darian lived in had become a disaster. It smelled like a stinky, musty, and stale man. I didn't want to sit down, but from the looks of things, I was very much needed. "You must have just passed out as soon as you made it home from work." I was curious of how Darian could have worked all day but was in such a deep sleep so quickly after getting home from work.

I felt like putting my foot in my mouth as I watched a once-strong man drop his head. An extremely ashamed Darian began to explain that he was on an administrative leave. He said that something went wrong with another project that he was over. Since this project resulted in a tragic mishap, an investigation was started. He said that it could take months for the case to be settled.

I was trying to understand, but I was wrapped around the fact that Darian had got himself out there so bad that he done messed up his good job. He wasn't a bum yet, but with his unshaven face and his see-through dreads, he did look like a crackhead. He was also full of excuses. Didn't he know that doing drugs was his choice? I knew that losing Catalina had driven him crazy, but to choose this life of hell is crazy.

Although I felt like giving up, I kept talking to Darian. I needed to know when, why, and how he started. First he tried denying his issue until I snapped out and told him that I knew all about the drug transactions that had transpired between him and my husband.

I wasn't completely sure if I was ready for it, but a devastated Darian spilled his guts. He explained that he had a drug addiction when he was sixteen. My heart almost jumped out of my body when he said that a guy named Z that was older than him convinced him to hang out. I knew that there could be more than one damn Z, but I was pretty sure that he was one in the same. I wondered if Darian knew that Z was out of jail, and that he was Zatron's daddy.

With sincere remorse, Darian went on to say that he didn't want to tell me about Caleb. After I explained to him that I was done with Caleb and his lies, he continued. He said that Caleb and Zatron popped up at his doorsteps one night, claiming that they wanted to kick it. Darian said that since he knew Caleb, that he didn't mind drinking some beer and watching some football. Being done with my husband felt even better when he said that Caleb and Zatron were smoking crack and pleaded with him to try it. "Fortunately, I was able to resist and I asked them to leave." I was relieved that Darian didn't smoke crack with them but was confused. When did he start? Knowing that I was waiting, Darian finished by telling me that he received a phone call from Cat, which led to an argument and her telling him that because of him, she could never conceive again.

When poor Darian told me that, he called them back to his house and smoked a chunk of his savings away. I was dumbfounded. I couldn't get over the fact that a man that I loved could be a part of such an ultimate deception.

I continued to listen to Darian, and as he pieced together the date of this deception, I realized that Z would have been out at that time. I asked Darian if he had seen Z. Darian's rattled mind remembered that he had indeed seen Z a couple of days prior to the boys showing up at his house. He then recalled that Z approached him while he was about to leave the store "Hey, pretty Ricky, look at you in your BMW." Darian said that he wanted no parts of Z, so he just returned the greeting and walked away.

"Damn, Nita, how did my life end up this way?" Poor Darian was a wreck. He went on and on about how he made one bad choice after the other. He repeatedly blamed himself for losing Catalina. I cried with him as he cried, "If I would have prayed harder and worked in the church with her, she might be with me now instead of a white foreigner."

It was hard for me to fight back my tears, but I managed to let Darian know that it wasn't his fault. I told him how Catalina always had a way of making those that love her feel that any disagreement with her would be their fault. I went on to say that when Cat became religious, she got worse. Catalina got so high that she needed us to serve her. I then just looked at Darian and wondered if Catalina knew that those little people like us, the sinners, choose to be lost than to listen to her preach about living right.

Darian and I were both an emotional wreck, and I couldn't leave him; so after telling Big Belle's worker to stay overnight, I decided to lift Darian's sprits. I started by cleaning up and fixing him a bite to eat. The poor guy looked like he had lost twenty pounds. It was a combination of crack and a broken heart.

After eating, Darian and I sat on the sofa and continued our conversation. He made a huge step by admitting that he was a crackhead. I was stunned as he told me how much he had spent on this habit. He also let me know that Caleb became his supplier after Zatron died. Then he started buying from Marcus Jr. I started to feel conquered as I thought about the cruelty of the world. My baby is selling crack to a man who had helped the both of us plenty of times. Darian noticed the wrinkle on my forehead and began to explain himself. "Nita, I know how this must sound, but please understand that I didn't go to Marcus until I got confirmation that I may lose my job or better yet go to jail."

I was so sympathetic to Darian's feelings that I allowed him to lay his head on my shoulder; well actually, he was closer to my bosom. As I pulled and twirled his spongy locks, he told me that he hadn't been touched that way in years. "Nita, you are so beautiful. You deserve a man that would love all of you." As Darian's voice became sexier, I found myself wanting to please him. I knew that I had always been attracted to him, but never thought of being intimate with my aunt's husband. Well, he is free now, I thought as I let Darian do things that only Caleb had done to me. In a matter of minutes, Darian made Caleb seem like an amateur. After hours, he had erased all other sexual encounters from my brain. Darian left me brain dead and speechless, so again I found myself hell bound.

When our sexual storm ceased, the surge of stimulating pleasures went a way as we realized who we were. I think that Darian felt as much shame as I did. Big Belle would have a hissy fit. The thought of Big Belle mad me guilty. I felt ashamed of being naked, so I covered myself. I also planned on staying all night but couldn't wait to get home. I had good intentions. My mind was dedicated to helping Darian face his demons and move forward. However, the many demons inside of me made me sashay around in front of a sex-deprived man that had hit rock bottom. My speeches of encouragement that were meant to help him work harder at life only encouraged him to work hard at getting me in the bed, which wasn't hard.

CHAPTER 20

I Am Big Belle

A few months had passed since my incident with Darian, and I was still on an emotional rollercoaster. I tried to block the horrible act of sin out of mind, but instead, I awaited punishment. God was always punishing me for something. I had started believing that he punished me because I had a need to do right consciously.

Divorcing Caleb also had me feel unrighteous. After finding out how he helped to deceive Darian, I could not keep my vows. He even taught my boy how to be a drug dealer. Caleb was responsible for me feeling that I had no choice but to let Marcus Jr. go live with his daddy.

My anger against Caleb helped me get over the fact that he would be in prison for several years. I told myself that divorcing him was for the best. I could never wait too many years for a nothing-ass nigga that didn't do right while he was out. He would most likely be gay anyway.

I'D RATHER GO TO HELL THAN THE HEAVEN THAT YOU'RE IN

Stressing over the men in my life was immediately put on the back burner as I was faced with the thought of losing my rock, Big Belle. The doctors told us that Big Belle would not live another year. I decided that I didn't want Big Belle to know what the doctor said, so everyone agreed to keep it from her. This was crazy since Big Belle didn't believe a doctor could control God's time. I didn't either, but I felt they were close with their educated guesses. Therefore, I took a leave from work to spend as much time as possible with Big Belle.

Every now and then, I got away from Big Belle. Since my uncle never moved in the ole house, I often went and checked on it. Sometimes I would sit and think about the good times. Big Belle hadn't been herself since leaving her home. I had taken some of her stuff to my house but left most of her boxed items there. While walking and sitting on Big Belle's ole bed, I decided to go through some of her things in search of ideas that may cheer her up during her last days.

One thing that caught my eye was a purse full of obituaries. I went through them and read a couple. However, I really wanted to read my momma's, but it wasn't there. When I was younger, I loved to read my name "Bonita had one child Zonita Labelle Walker." Confused of where it could be, I began looking through other things in Big Belle's clutter. In the midst of so much junk, I found a box of journals. Full of suspense, I nosed through a few of them and found that they were full of poems written by Big Belle.

After an hour of excitement, I came across a poem that blew my mind. I had never read this poem before, but it was almost identical to a piece I wrote when I was in jail.

DEAD ENDS

I HATE WHEN I GO TO A PLACE THAT
I'VE BEEN OVER AND OVER AGAIN

GET IN A HURRY AND FORGET THAT
THIS ROAD LEADS TO A DEAD END

I CAN'T BELIEVE THE SITUATION
THAT I KEEP PUTTING MYSELF IN

DEAD ENDS ARE BECOMING A TREND

I BET IF YOU HAVE PATIENCE
YOU COULD FIGURE OUT

THERE HAS TO BE ANOTHER ROUTE

THERE IS A REASON WHY THEY SAY

GOOD THINGS COME TO THOSE WHO WAIT

LEAVE EARLY IF YOU ARE ALWAYS RUNNING LATE

THINGS WILL GO AND LOOK A
LITTLE SMOOTHER IF YOU TAKE
SOME WEIGHT OFF YOUR PLATE

A DEAD END MAY BE THE END IF
YOU CONTINUE AT YOUR RATE

WHAT IS A DEAD END

A PLACE WHERE YOU GO AND GO
THEM YOU CAN'T GO NO MOE

AS A BEAUTICIAN IT'S WHEN YOUR HAIR GROW
AND GROW THEN CAN'T GROW NO MORE.

I TAKE OUT MY SCISSORS, NOT TO OFFEND

BUT TO RID YOU OF THOSE DEAD ENDS.

Reminiscing in the old house did my heart some good. I felt more of Big Belle's spirit there than I did at home in the same room with her. She was getting so weak, and I realized that she would be better off going home to her Jesus.

On the way home, I couldn't stop thinking about Big Belle's writings. I decided to bring them home with me so that I could read them all and remind Big Belle of them. I also couldn't wait to read my poem "Dead Ends" to her so that she could see how alike our minds were. I was surprised that she never gave me this box of journals herself.

When I got back, Big Belle's aide told me that Big Belle had instructed her to call all of her kids. She said that Big Belle told her that the book of numbers was on her nightstand but that she just couldn't find it. After I calmed her and let her know that I had taken it and that

I would call them for Big Belle, she let me know that Big Belle wanted them to come to my house for Sunday dinner.

Hearing this news, I knew that I had to fulfill what may be Big Belle's final wish. She loved all her children even if they said that she had picks. Maybe this is why she wanted them to come. If she tells them "I love you" one more time, it may sink through. She would always be my Big Belle, so who cared about them.

Aunt Margaret and Aunt Nicety were the easiest to convince. Of course, Aunt Margaret's negative response was "Is momma getting ready to die?" I used a suck-up method with Catalina. I told her that Big Belle needed her strongest child to be present at this celebration dinner. I was lying through my teeth but had to get her on board somehow. She even took over and went out of her way to get the other siblings to come even if she had to provide transportation.

The week flew by, and Sunday was here. I had worked all week preparing to fix all Big Belle's requested foods. The menu consisted of everything from ham hocks and beans to crackling bread with turnip greens. The only thing I disobeyed her on was the chitterlings. I liked them but refused to have them stinky things in my beautiful home.

Just when I started thinking I had everything under control, Big Belle, who hadn't walked in years, came walking into the kitchen. In total shock, I hurried and grabbed her ole cane. She was as spunky as I had seen in forever. It felt good to hear her snap on me for being so scared and to tell me that I better stir the dumplings before they stick. She then mumbled, "Where is everybody?"

"Ain't I enough for you? We can eat all this food by ourselves."

As I was bragging about how pretty my caramel cake was, Catalina came in, fussing, "Mother, how are you? What are you doing out the bed?" Big Belle seemed to be her ole self when she put Cat in check "Wait a minute now. Last time I checked, I was your mother." It felt wonderful to be laughing at Big Belle again.

I was so relieved that all of Big Belle's kids made it. Uncle Jimmy was violating parole, but oh well, he went to jail for dumb shit; at least this time, he would be going for his momma. Anyway, everyone was in good spirits, which pleased Big Belle's spirits. So after our bellies and hearts were full from food and laughter, Big Belle said that it was time for a little church. I don't know how she done, it but she preached a sermon. The doors of the church were opened right there in my house. Big Belle got through to all of us. Aunt Margaret was speaking in tongues, and it didn't seem fake.

We stayed up really late, and I couldn't believe that Big Belle just kept on praising God and being an inspiration to all of us. She had such a way with words. I loved to hear her speak about any and everything. This reminded me of how sad it felt at the thought of her leaving this world. "Who would keep her legacy alive? Who would continue spitting her rhymes?" Just when I thought that I had heard them all, she would throw a new one out there. When everybody was complimenting my peach cobbler, Big Belle said, "If a girl can't bake, then her house won't shake." Like most of her rhymes, I had to think twice about the meaning. However, when I got it, I laughed my butt off.

I hadn't planned for everyone to stay at my house, but just like the ole days, everyone found a spot. I gave up my room and decided to sleep in the room with Big Belle. When I was a child, that was my safe place. While I was in her room, I wasn't scared of being haunted by the spirits of the house. I felt safe because of Big Belle's prayers. She always got on her knees and prayed for several minutes before going to sleep. I also learned to pray but did it in the bed. I was too scared that a mouse would be on the floor.

This particular night, I slept in Big Belle's rocking chair as peaceful as a baby. My dreams were pleasant but strange. I dreamed that I had a baby. In the dream, I walked around the ole house holding a bright-skinned little baby boy. I was walking and searching for Big Belle to pray for him, but I couldn't find her. The louder the baby cried, the louder I cried, "Big Belle." Next thing I knew, I was awake and still crying out, "Big Belle." I then rose quickly to check on her.

Big Belle made a peaceful exit from this world. She made sure that we all felt the peace. So instead of crying tears of sorrow, I cried tears of joy. Yes, my rock was gone, but she made sure that she left enough knowledge behind of hers and our solid rock.

The peace immediately left when Catalina arrived to discuss arrangements, and who would get Big Belle's things. Everybody knew that Big Belle didn't have a will; she always said that those were for rich white folks. She probably figured that it wouldn't be hard to decide what to do with her few possessions. The ole house would be for any family member who needed to live there, and as for her Bibles and journals, I already have claims on them.

I couldn't believe it when Catalina suggested that Big Belle's funeral be held at one of her big fancy churches. Her reasons were good, "It's free and there is plenty of room." However, I could never forget Big Belle's funeral talks. This is when she would tell me that I better make sure that she was pretty and that the service wasn't too long. She definitely mentioned her church being her home-going venue.

I must have had some Big Belle in me because I was able to convince everyone to do things my way. So with little time, the funeral was planned. Uncle Paul decided to move in to the house and be responsible for the upkeep. As for her clothes, the girls would get what they wanted. All she had was church dresses and heels, but they were sharp. Big Belle was a woman with a lot of fashion sense.

It was easy for me to pick her white-and-silver suit to bury her in since she often commented that she looked so good in that suit that she wanted to wear it all the time. She did look like an angel whenever she wore it. As for her hair, she used to wear wigs, but after going through my hair treatment program, her hair had grown enough to be worn in a classy short style. It was a style that she always hinted that she would love having. Her silver hair sparkled as I froze it in place for the last time.

The funeral home people probably thought I was crazy as I talked to Big Belle. "Girl, your hair is fried, dyed, and laid to the side just like momma used to do it. I figured since you going to see her, you should look like she done your hair." This was the only way that I was going to get through this day. I laughed like Big Belle was going to laugh back.

Although I agreed to be on the program for a tribute, I hadn't come up with anything. I had until morning to come up with something, and each time I thought I had something, it was shut down. I knew that I couldn't let Big Belle go out like that. I needed something that would touch everyone's hearts just like Big Belle did.

After saying my prayer that night before the early afternoon home going of my momma Big Belle, I decided to sleep. I figured God would lead me in what to say that morning. I was not at all surprised when I tossed and turned for hours. When I did finally doze off, I was awakened by a deep moaning cry coming from downstairs. It sounded like Marcus Jr., but he wasn't due in until time for the funeral.

Look at my baby, I thought as I saw it was him sitting on Big Belle's bed, crying like a baby. Marcus Jr. hugged me and cried harder. He believed that it was his fault that Big Belle died. He also was consumed with guilt because he didn't get to see her first. At that moment, I knew that I had to become strong for my son. "Look at me, boy. Your grandma would tell you that she is not gone, she just getting some beauty rest. She would also tell you that she is waiting on us. All we have to do is live like she did for Jesus, and one day we will again rest next to her."

For the first time in a long time, my son listened to me. He dried his tears and said that he was going to do better for Big Belle's sake. He didn't say for Jesus's sake, but it was a start.

After putting my big teenager boy to sleep, I was wired and ready to write my tribute. I grabbed one of Big Belle's journals and went through it briefly. My finger stopped when I got to a poem titled "My Testimony." It started with such a strong question, "What do you see when you look at me?" It then goes on to say, "I hope you see a woman that has always let God take the lead." The ending of the poem was powerful. It said, "I hope you see a woman that is always ready to give a testimony."

I was in another world at Big Belle's funeral. Up until they called my name for a tribute, I had been praying, asking God to give me the right words to say. As I walked to the front of the church, my spirit said, "What would Big Belle say?" When I made it to the front of the church, I felt a circle of heat surrounding my body. The closer I got to the casket, the warmer I felt. Totally out of my body, I began to speak with an old gospel moan in my voice, "I'm fired up. I'm wired up and with Jesus. I'm going higher up. As you look at this casket, don't you cry over me. Remember, I borrowed this body. Thank God for letting me use it and make it on time. You see if you make it, everything will be fine. Use your borrowed gift for the ministry of Christ as I done with mine. You can't sit there like you are through. As long as you are breathing, you have work to do. Study Genesis to the Book of Revelation, and then you will understand your connection. Then ask yourself how can you stop others from wanting to go in the opposite direction?" Then I spoke, "If you live like Big Belle, all is well. No one will think that your heaven is on the same level as hell."

By this time, the music was playing, the drums were pounding, and the mother's had gathered around me doing the Big Belle's praise dance. As I moved my feet, I could feel my butt moving like Big Belle's used to. I looked at my shadow on the wall, and I saw Big Belle. At first I felt spooked but realized that it was my shadow. I am Big Belle.

CHAPTER 21

True Love

A few months after losing Big Belle, I learned that I was going to have my second child. I was devastated. Here I was pregnant and not sure, but most likely, it was Darian's baby. If Big Belle wasn't already dead, the news of me sleeping with Cat's first love would have killed her. How do I know? I knew because it was killing me.

I had been going to church every Sunday. I even sung in the choir trying to do what the Lord said. Now you punish me by letting me have another baby with no husband? Yes, I had sex with Darian, but I would never marry my aunt's ex-husband. Yes, she was a bitch, but I loved her. She may be over Darian by mouth, but deep in her heart, she still loves him.

The thought of sleeping with Darian that night and now carrying his child had me feeling guilty. I felt like running away. I didn't want

Cat to see my baby boy and think of hers. I knew it was a boy and that he would look just like Darian. I dreamed it.

It felt like deja vu when Darian showed up at my doorstep. I hurried and put on a big sweatshirt before letting him in. Last thing I needed was his suspicions. I hadn't seen Darian since Big Belle's funeral, and I can't recall if I even spoke with him.

The last thing I expected to hear out of Darian's mouth was a testimony. He told me how thankful he was that I helped him. He said that he had been in a rehab for the past few months. He then went on to ecstatically say that his boss pulled some strings and got the case against him dismissed. I was happy for Darian but felt confusion as he told me that he and Catalina were getting back together.

Apparently, Cat admitted to Darian that she buried herself into that church stuff to avoid her own disastrous life. She spent years of ministering to others before she realized how she needed to be. She had read the entire Bible but never connected herself to it.

Darian never looked happier as he told me that Catalina said that she could never love another man. She said that knowing that she could never give him a child because she argued over a dumb house, put her into a deep depression of denial. In the end, Catalina didn't blame him, she blamed herself.

By the time Darian left, I was so mixed up in my mind that I had put my faith on the back burner once again. I couldn't believe that Catalina's life was coming back together, and mine was again ruined. Well, mine had never been together. "I will always be a nothing-ass woman with no husband." My attitude about life was "no life."

At Catalina's wedding, I was due any day. I managed to make everyone think it was Caleb's baby so that I could at least show my face. I'm glad that I got to go to the wedding and glad that this couple that was meant to be were reunited. Their wedding vows were so deep that only a fool couldn't see that this was true love.

I had never felt so alone in my life. There I lay, giving birth to a beautiful little boy with no support. I didn't even feel the pain of giving birth, most likely because I had such a heavy pain in my heart. My heavy heart became cold toward my baby. I couldn't stand to look at him and told the nurses to keep him. I knew that I would be keeping him all by myself soon enough. I then drifted off to sleep, hoping that I would see Big Belle. My life was hell. I needed her.

The next morning, as I was preparing to go home, Catalina showed up with some "It's a boy" balloons and all kinds of gifts. I was already guilty, but it was worse when she began to cry and pour her heart out to me. She said that she never hated me, and that she was envious of me for having children and for being more like Big Belle than any of her children.

All this time I had been wanting to be like her, and she wanted what I had. This was all too crazy to me. I began to wonder if Cat knew my secret, would she forgive me? This was far worse than when I burned her red pants. Too bad I wasn't still a teenager. Life is very real once you get older.

I was very grateful to Cat for helping the baby and I get settled in at home. The entire time that she helped me, she had a very genuine smile. I guess she was happy that I let her name the baby. I hadn't given much thought to a name, so when she suggested Unis, I went along with it. She wanted to name him something that reminded us of the new unity that had happened in our family.

Unis Walker was the name of her husband's son. Cat even suggested that she and Darian become little Unis's godparents. Life couldn't get more complicated for me than at this very moment. I knew then that I had yet another secret to take to the grave. Lies couldn't get you to heaven, but I didn't want to get any closer to hell than I was right now.

I'D RATHER GO TO HELL THAN THE HEAVEN THAT YOU'RE IN

CHAPTER 22

The Truth

Unis was a good baby. All he did was eat and sleep. I had a lot time on my hands. The shop called often but with quick-to-answer questions. I didn't know if I was having postpartum depression or if I was just overwhelmed. I did feel better in the evenings when I drank hot tea and read another one of Big Belle's journals. Reading about her perspective in life helped me learn even more from her after death.

After hours of reading, I felt sleepy. However, after reading the title page of the last journal that I opened, I was wide awake. This was a letter not a poem, and it was addressing me. "To my little girl Zonita." I then hurried through a couple of pages to see why Big Belle would write me a letter. To my surprise, this journal was not written by Big

Belle. It was written by my momma Bonita Walker. Full of suspense, I started over and read slowly.

The letter started by saying that if I was reading this than she was probably in heaven. She explained her actions got her in way over her head. She explained how there were these men that were trying to kill her and her boyfriend Z. Z apparently took the blame and was hated by her brothers. Her brothers promised to kill Z if he didn't stay away. When the smoke seemed to clear the air, she decided the hell with her brothers and let Z come back around after I was almost two. She pretended that she hadn't been with him to conceive me.

"His name is Zatron Mackley. Zonita, he is your daddy." She went on to say that if she was killed, that he probably disappeared to protect you from being killed. Momma went on to say that he loved me from the first time that he laid eyes on me. He vowed to protect his little girl from all harm.

While reading this, my body became chilled, and I had a memory that I had repeatedly my entire life. I remembered being covered by a man while the firecrackers popped. That's why I hated the Fourth of July. I knew now that the man was my daddy. He saved me just like he did at his coming home party. Z knew that it was me, and so he disappeared to save me just like he did years ago.

After crying and reading the rest of momma's journal, I realized how she was just like me. Her short-lived life was full of hell just like mine was. Just like me, she tried to pray like Big Belle taught her, and she tried to keep faith. Her biggest request to God was to let me live and to let me become the woman she never got to become. Then there was more about how she hoped that I would listen to Big Belle and do the right thing even when it felt unbearable.

I knew from my momma's letter just what I had to do. I had to tell Cat and Darian the truth; even if she hated me afterwards. I was so thankful that my momma's prayer kept me alive that I was ready to give myself completely back to God. He had just given me a miracle "The truth". Now I needed to tell the TRUTH.

CHAPTER 23

The Sermon

The baby was about to turn one, and I had decided to have a big party. The first thing I did was invite the whole family. Next, I decided to let the godparents have it at their home. My final plan would be the big surprise, which was telling Cat and Darian the truth before the party started.

Darian and Catalina were stronger than ever. They had become members of Big Belle's old church too. Darian had been called to the ministry while Catalina had decided to serve as the first lady. It took a lot of guts for her to give up her power and be under her husband. It seemed like every Sunday, they were up talking about forgiveness, so I figured they should be ready to forgive the unforgiveable. So on my baby's birthday, I planned to give him a gift, his daddy.

Unis and I arrived at Catalina and Darian's house a few hours before the party would start. They were so happy to see us. Catalina was walking on clouds just like she was back when she and Darian first fell in love. I didn't want to burst their bubble, but it was time that the truth came out. Since Catalina had been betrayed by me the most, I decided to tell her first.

After talking Darian in to taking the baby out to play, I asked Cat to sit and chat with me for a minute. With a tremor in my voice, I began to first explain how it all happened and what had happened between Darian and me. I figured I would explain the first betrayal, which led to the second one.

Before I could get my first sentence out, Catalina stopped me and said, "Nita, I already know about it." She then went on to tell me that Darian and her decided to make sure they had no skeletons before moving forward. She told me that she forgave me and loved me with all her heart. She then told me that the flesh becomes so weak, and that it was normal because of Adam and Eve in the garden. She said that, eventually, people have to understand that forgiving someone is always hard, but to remember that through Jesus, God forgives us of much worse, and every day we betray him with our sinful ways.

I was so relieved that I didn't have to tell Cat about Darian and me sleeping together. At least my second betrayal wouldn't seem so bad. "That's not all, Cat," I mumbled. "There is another secret that I have been keeping from the both of you." This time Darian walked in with Unis in his arms and interrupted. He told me that he knew that Unis was his from the first time he laid eyes on him. He told me that because he was so grateful to me for helping him that he would wait for me to come to them when I was ready.

Catalina swallowed hard, like "I don't know about a baby," but she handled it well; and for once in my life, I felt complete. Seeing Darian with Unis made me decide to let Unis spend so much time with him and Cat that they would think he was both of theirs. Wow, God does work in mysterious ways, I thought as I was again in agreement with Big Belle.

The party was a huge success. Unis had everything. His white side of the family even came. Darian had invited them all, knowing that

Unis was more than a godson. Personally, I was glad that he decided to hold off on letting them know about Unis. I would have felt so out of place being looked at as a mistress.

Some people like Mrs. Polkey would be very judgmental. Catalina would have to invite her. She was getting old and senile. Every Sunday at church, she cries about her friend Belle. Mrs. Polkey may have been a nosey, hypocritical lady to us when we were younger, but at least she taught us that faithfulness to the church meant a lot.

On Sunday morning, the church was packed. Marcus Jr. was home visiting and even decided to go. The song that Catalina opened church with was a powerful worship song. "No matter what you're going through, Jesus will see you through, so look to the skies, and he will hear your cries. He will turn your old day into a new day. He'll turn your old ways into new ways." The whole church waved their hands and sung along.

Darian's sermon was exactly what the church folk needed especially me. I was a member of the church but had not been doing as I should. I would always get mad at some of the old folks and stay away for months, sometimes years. Anyway, his sermon was called "the tools of a growing church." He let us know what each of us needed to do in order to help the church grow. He preached about several things, but what stood out most to me was when he said that our actions inside and outside the church pushes young people away. He said that if we can't learn to keep a smile on our face and let our lights shine, that people wouldn't look to us for help. Therefore, they turn to the streets, which is what the devil wants. The drug dealers and the night club owners are the ones that are smiling at our youth and our lost people. They sell them a fake dream. "You all should live the ultimate dream. Walk like a saint of God. Talk like a saint of God. Be a faithful saint of God, and those that are lost will follow you to Christ."

As Darian concluded his sermon, the music got louder, and the people were chanting, "Say it, brother. Halleluiah! Amen." He then sang a song that allowed him to open up the doors of the church, "God Is Waiting for You." I was so thankful that God had waited on me, that I gave Marcus Jr. the baby while I went to the Lord. I was willing and able to do whatever it was that he needed me to do.

When Catalina hugged me, I felt the Holy Spirit move all through me. "Thank you, Jesus," I cried. "Thank ya!" I sounded just like Big Belle. I even felt like I was her. Everything that she had taught me came flowing through my brain. I began to understand why she shouted around the church. At this time, I knew why she didn't worry about the bad things that we would face. I also knew why she wasn't afraid to die. She didn't die; she went to live somewhere where there is no pain, no starvation, and no bills. She went to glory.

CHAPTER 24

My Calling

Nine years of my life flew by, but not before I went through countless trials and tribulations. Throughout these nine years, I had managed to stay on the Lord's side. Don't get me wrong. I did get off the path several times, but when I thought about his goodness, I prayed my way back.

Marcus Jr. was twenty-six-years-old now and had spent a few years in prison for involuntary man slaughter. When he was twenty-one, he refused to listen to any of us. I preached to him that his temper would eventually get him in trouble one of these days. Sure enough, he let this dude push his buttons. He told me, "Momma, you don't understand. Dude had a gun, so I had to beat him down." I was so mad, so I fussed. "If he had a gun, he could have killed you!" My next and really my only option was to put it in God's hands. I told him to pray every day, and he would be out before he knew it. He did get out, and Darian gave him a job that he has been working at for a whole year now. He was so proud of himself, and so was I.

Unis was ten now and had grown to be such a well-mannered kid. I gave Cat and Darian all the credit. They kept him all summer long, some holidays, and any other time that they wanted. By the grace of God, we were able to raise him without him wondering why I slept with my aunt's husband.

Darian and Catalina were still strong. The church was thriving. It had one of the largest memberships ever. It was remodeled two years ago to accommodate the large membership. It was very fancy but was still full of soulful spirits. If you listened hard, I believed that you could hear Big Belle's voice coming through the ceiling. Well, at least I could. Maybe I was hearing myself.

The new church was a beautiful venue for Caleb's and my wedding. Caleb had been out of prison for a few years now. He had been very forgiving of me for divorcing him and for having another baby. He worked extra hard to prove that he had been rehabilitated in order to get me back. He got his barber license while he was in prison, which allowed him to work in our shop. God had blessed me to stop claiming everything was mine and to help someone else with my blessings. Caleb and I worked peacefully together until I became pregnant with Bella.

Bella is Caleb's and my daughter that was born a year ago. I didn't think I would be forty-five having a baby, but God had other plans. We were so blessed that Bella was born with no problems. Big Belle used to say that old folks have old babies with issues, but not my Bella, She was perfect.

Z, my daddy, was in his sixties and finally free. The people that wanted him dead were no longer an issue. God handled them! As for Z and I, we became close. I forgave him for his bad choices in life. He was so grateful that he went to church every Sunday and spent as much time with us as he could. We talked about Zatron Jr. a lot, which helped us deal with him being gone. I was sad that I didn't get to know Zatron Jr. as a brother but grateful that I knew him.

As for me, I spent all my extra time writing. While I was on maternity leave, I reread all of Big Belle's and my momma's journals. They were full of encouragement. I had read them before, but each time I reread them, it was like reading the Bible. I always learned something new.

There was a poem in my Mother's book called "Dance with Me."

DANCE WITH ME

I LOVE CHURCH AND I LIKE THE CLUB TOO.
ADMITTING TO WHAT YOU LIKE
SAYS A LOT ABOUT YOU.
WHEN I'M IN THE CHURCH, THE SPIRIT OF THE
LORD LETS ME SPEAK, HIS FIRE MAKES ME MOVE.
WHEM I'M IN THE CLUB, I SIP
WINE SO I CAN GROOVE.
MUSIC SO LOUD, I CAN'T HEAR MYSELF TALK
SO I CONCENTRATE ON MY HIGH-HEELED WALK
THERE YA'LL GO TALKING, I KNOW
YA'LL USED TO CUT A RUG
NOW YOU ARE PERFECT AND
YOU ARE THE JUDGE.

THERE IS NOTHING BUT DEVILS IN THEM CLUBS

SHOOTING, KILLINGS
AND DRUG DEALINGS
I LOVE CHURCH, I'M LEARNING
TO PUT GOD FIRST
BUT NOW I AM STRESSED BECAUSE
I WORE THIS SKIRT
THEY SHAKING THEIR HEADS LIKE I'M DIRT
LOOK AT HER IN THAT TIGHT SKIRT
SHE CAME TO CHURCH JUST TO
MAKE OUR MEN FLIRT
SHE A JESABELLE
ON HER WAY TO HELL
THERE YA'LL GO WITH YOUR NOSE IN
THE AIR AND BAD IS ALL YOU SMELL

I'D RATHER GO TO HELL THAN THE HEAVEN THAT YOU'RE IN

BUT IT IS YOU WITH THE LIFE THAT STINKS
YOU KNOW THE LORD BUT LET THE
DEVIL CONTROL WHAT YOU THINK
YOUR FROWN SO STIFF YOU CAN'T BLINK
IN THE TEMPLE GOD SHOULD
BE ON YOUR MIND
ALL THE TIME
THEN SHE MAY GET SAVED EVEN IF
SHE IS SHOWING HER BEHIND
I LIKE THE CLUB I DRESS TO IMPRESS
SOME OF THEM GIRLS TALKING
BECAUSE THEY LOOK A MESS
SCARED 'CAUSE HIS EYES FIXATED ON MY DRESS.
I DON'T EVEN WANT HER MAN,
I WANT ONE FOR MYSELF
I KNOW THERE HAS TO BE ONE LEFT
NOW I'M FEELING THIS WINE
SO IT'S ABOUT THAT TIME
I GET IN THE MIRROR LOOK AT MINE
AND MOVE TO THE MUSIC UNTIL
MY BODY UNWINDS
I LOVE GOD SO BACK TO CHURCH I GO
LOOK AROUND AND I SEE THE EYES ROLL
SURELY THEY MUST BELIEVE
THAT I'M NOT A HOE
BUT IT REALLY DOESN'T MATTER
WHAT THEY THINK THEY KNOW
I MUST CLEAR MY MIND
IT'S PRAYING TIME
WHEN THE MIC IS PASSED MY WAY
I WILL HAVE ALREADY PRAYED
THAT I BE USED AS A VESSEL TODAY
EVEN IF YOU DON'T WANT TO LOVE THE
SPIRIT OF GOD WILL MAKE YOU ANYWAY
SO EVEN IF HER SKIRT IS TIGHT, LET'S PRAISE
HIM THROUGH THE CIRCUMSTANCE

'CAUSE ALL SHE WANTED TO DO WAS DANCE.

–Bonita Walker

My momma's poem blew me away over and over again. Each time I read it, I understood more of it. With prayer, I began to understand what my calling was and how it was connected to this poem. I began to remember my momma's prayer to God, the one where she asked him to bless me to be the woman that she wanted to be. Her poem told me that she wanted to show people that being judgmental would push people away from the church and that everybody needed a church. Big Belle's writings taught me that although some people are judgmental, we must still learn to make better choices. In the end, it is our choice that determines rather we go to heaven or hell.

I was full of the spirit and very proud when they introduced me, Zonita Labelle Walker, as the speaker of the evening. It was my honor to speak at the commencement ceremony for the class of 2020.

By the time I got to the reason why I became determined to keep young girls and guys from choosing a bad place in life instead of going to a good place with me because of my snooty or other inconsiderate actions, everyone were on their feet. I wanted to talk about God, and that the good and bad places were heaven and hell, but the schools didn't allow any religious talk, not even a prayer. Still I was determined to somehow get my point across to hundreds of young adults. I needed our future church to know that I remember when I'd rather go to hell than the heaven that you are in.

PROLOGUE

I hope that you were uplifted and motivated to get through anything that is thrown your way during this journey called life. I believe that we all have or still have a Big Belle in our lives. Big Belle is someone who decided to run on and see what the end will be. She had enough strength to pray when others were too weak. She didn't give up on her faith so that those that she loved would eventually grab on to the legacy that she left behind.

The reason I chose to tell this story through the eyes of Zonita, whose character, at some point in time reminded me of different females in my life including myself, was to reach out to struggling youngsters; those that are overwhelmed with life. They spend more time expecting the bad than enjoying the good. Enjoying the good things that have been given to us can be difficult when we are never thankful of the simple things in life. When Zonita became thankful for what she went through, she was finally brought out. She thought she knew it all, but she didn't have a clue of God's wonderful plan. She grew up with hatred in her heart because people didn't do her right. However, she ended up having to love through her pain, and she learned that the sun seems even brighter after the rain.

Sometimes, we, as human beings, need a scapegoat. We need someone to blame for our shortcomings. If we decide to do something to better ourselves, like going to church, and things don't go the way we expect it, we blame others. It feels good to say the reason why I stop going to my drug abuse meetings was because of so-and-so. Now ask yourself this, Is so-and-so's organs in your body? Is it their responsibility to feed your children? Your answer should be no. Catalina's character was used as a person who became a scapegoat. After Zonita realized that her bad choices were of her own doings and no one was responsible for pushing her to do them, she became a Big Belle. Catalina also became a Big Belle.

We all have our own unique ways of becoming a Big Belle, but in the end, we must realize that we all have the same goal in life.

How much money we make, how many children we have, and so on are not a part of the ultimate goal. The ultimate goal is adjusting our attitudes and our actions toward the obstacles of this world so that we will be prepared to exit with those left here, knowing that our direction is heaven bound.

Bonita's character was used to show how your choices can affect the lives of your love one's even from the grave. Because she chose to do certain things, people looked at her child and never let go of Bonita's bad actions. I waited and used Jack to shed some light on Bonita so that I could show how people will hang on to the bad and act like no good ever existed. Until Zonita could be thankful for the fact that her momma was her momma no matter what, she struggled with her identity. She felt doomed and defeated, which was siding with the devil.

The men in Zonita's life also played a big part in this story. As a young girl, she battled with the fact that she didn't have a father. Her mother was dead, but Big Belle tried filling that void. Jack had been labeled as not good enough to be a father, so he chose not to be one. Darian became the first man in her life. All she knew was that when she got her first man that she wanted him to be perfect just like

Cat's Darian. I think that most of us can remember that when we were teenagers, no matter how many distractions we had like school and sports, we couldn't keep our minds off of finding that special someone. Relationships became extremely difficult for Zonita because she was worried that she wasn't living up to expectations that she had set for herself. It took years of spiritual growth before she could have what she always wanted in a man.

What I loved most about my story was the fact that after all the crying and laughing that you go through as you read about Zonita's life struggles was the excitement of how holding on to God's hand can lift you up and set you on top of a sinful world. Meaning that one day, if you believe, you can leave all the bad past behind and live an abundant, peaceful life.

ABOUT THE AUTHOR

Jerri Locke was born in Chicago, Illinois. Immediately after birth she returned to Tamms, Illinois where she was raised and currently resides. Jerri is the oldest of four children. She has two younger brothers and one sister.

Jerri describes her childhood as one that was torn between two families that were linked together by marriage and her. She loved both sides, but often became discouraged when one side would make fun of her for having characteristics of the other. This caused her to have a very interesting, but challenging childhood. Growing up no one listened to her when she tried to express her feelings, so writing was always her only outlet.

Jerri did not get to enjoy becoming a teenager because at age 15 she became pregnant. She had her first daughter at age 16, finishing high school with all A's along with many other exceptional accomplishments. She was a cheerleader, basketball, and softball player. She also received numerous awards in state competitions for writing essays and speeches.

After high school Jerri attended four years of college, but received no degree. Instead, she fell in love and had another daughter at age 22. Jerri spent the next few years raising two children alone with a husband in prison.

A couple years later, Jerri gets a divorce and later remarries. She seems to have it all this time. She is struck with another obstacle in her life when she loses a son at 36 weeks pregnant. Jerri decides to have another child, a girl who is now 7.

Her second husband left 5 years ago causing Jerri to turn to writing to express her anger and disappointments. She wrote a poetry book full of issues in her life that needed to be said. Jerri turned her infamous poetry book into a novel. She is now a successful beautician and author.

To.
Tessi
I hope that
you are inspired
by my every word!!!
Thanks
Author Ginger